Finch Books by L.S. Barron

Single Books
Adorned in Blood

ADORNED IN BLOOD

L.S. BARRON

Adorned in Blood
ISBN # 978-1-83943-961-2
©Copyright L.S. Barron 2021
Cover Art by Louisa Maggio ©Copyright March 2021
Interior text design by Claire Siemaszkiewicz
Finch Books

Published in 2021 by Finch Books, United Kingdom.

Finch Books is an imprint of Totally Entwined Group Limited.

ADORNED IN BLOOD

Chapter One

Streams of Crimson Blood

The golden rays from the alleyway streetlamp glimmered through the mist and fog. The drizzly rain fell lightly upon my eyelashes. I felt the coldness as it wreaked an ill chill through my body. Somehow, the thirst had taken over once again. Everything else in my mind had been put aside.

The back door of the diner opened. It was a shabby place—hardly even a rat dared linger there, except the rat that ran the place. There in the mist was the man himself, throwing out the night's garbage into the already rank alleyway. He was a savage of a being. He was mean to my kind, mean to all kinds.

"Hey, kid, what are you doing back here?" the crotchety man asked.

I wiped the rain from my eyes. The saliva ran down the side of my mouth. *Attack!*

It was soon over. I so liked the color blue and how it looked on me. I thought it brought out more of the blue in my hazel eyes. Almost all my shirts were some shade of blue. *Dang, I shouldn't have worn my favorite.*

The blue T-shirt had streams of crimson red blood running down it, like it was a newly designed pattern, meant to be that way.

The savage lay at my feet, lifeless. *No more will he be unkind to me…or to anyone, for that matter.* I pushed the man's side with my sneaker to make sure he was now lifeless. There was no movement, no breath. Dead.

I wiped the blood from my face on my arm. I looked up into the drizzly rain, letting it rinse my face clean, erasing my sinful act. I admired the rays of light from the streetlamp. I felt pure, rejuvenated. I was not mournful for the beast of a man. There was no regret. I felt renewed and fell into a deep, restful sleep.

My alarm clock sounded. Morning had quickly arrived, with the memories of the night only a fleeting moment in my mind. The school day ahead was not what I was worried about. I combed my now short blondish-brown hair as I stood in front of my bedside mirror. I glanced down at one of my old swimming trophies. 'High Point Award, 9–10 girls, Jenna Holliday'. *Jenna Michelle Holliday, hmm…* I chuckled. Yes, that once had been my name. Now, however, it is simply Michael Holliday.

I repeated that in the mirror out loud. "Michael Holliday."

The name flowed so much better off my tongue. It felt right. It felt comfortable, fitting.

When did I know that I was Michael and not that lost girl Jenna? Probably before I even had memories. My mom told me that by the time I was two, I had already started showing preferences toward the other gender. She told me that I would just drag my doll around by its hair like I hated the thing. Then I would fight the neighbor boy for his Matchbox trucks.

In my memory, I'd known by kindergarten at least. I'd known for sure dresses were out. All I'd wanted to wear were jeans and a T-shirt so that I could play roughhousing games with the boys any chance I got. I'd loved to fight, play football and wrestle. I'd wanted everything in a boy's life. I'd found no use for my girlie body and didn't feel like it belonged to me. I'd kept it at a distance, almost, like looking into the mirror and not seeing my real self.

Things have changed now. I was F2M post-op, at least the top half of my body, which I now loved. I was going to leave the lower stuff alone for now. Mom and Dad had been super supportive, so that was pretty cool, not like some kids who I've seen struggling. I'm on the T — testosterone injections. I was starting to finally show some facial scruff. That was pretty sick. I could do without the excessive underarm odor, but that was what Axe was for, I guessed. I have noticed of late that my shoulders are getting broader, but I also work out in the gym pretty hard.

However, right now, besides all this, I have this new thing to deal with. It's not like being sixteen brings enough problems already. Now I'm cursed with this bloodthirst too. I can't even remember who did this to me, but I'll find out. I'm going to have my revenge!

I had my suspects. Number one on my list? Mr. Drakon Branikov, my high school's history teacher. I think he's from Bulgaria — or maybe Hungary. I'm not sure, but he's definitely *not* from around here.

Mr. Branikov has long hair that he keeps pulled back in a ponytail and dark brown eyes, almost black. I feel like he could stare into my soul, though the girls seem to gaze at him in adoration. He dresses strangely, almost old-style, yet he seems young. That brought another question to my mind. *Why does he always seem to look the same age?* Other teachers had gotten older over the years. Not Mr. Branikov. I had lived in this town all my life. I had paid attention. This teacher was *not* what he seemed.

I had permission that night to go out with friends after the high-school football game. My plan, though, was something completely different. I would follow my suspect.

There had been criminals missing around town. There had been missing girls, not schoolgirls but ladies of the night, the skanky kind. I had done my research at the library. It seemed that the local papers showed that there had been several unsolved deaths and missing persons in recent years. Guess what? All since Mr. Branikov and his family had moved into town.

It seemed the cops didn't care much. Why would they? The town was becoming a safer and nicer place to live.

It had been a while since anyone had been missing or killed. I figured, if Mr. Branikov was like me, it was time to rejuvenate. I knew I could go a month or so, but not much longer. I didn't know about Mr. Branikov. *Is he an old Nosferatu? Did he draw the blood from my body first? Did he cause my thirst? Why?*

This notion that one should be moral and only live on animals? Yeah, that didn't work. I'd tried. No, only the pulsating blood of a human would suffice. So, I'd choose the most immoral beings that I could find — at least I'd try.

This would be a good night to feed. Town would be busy. Lowlifes would be crawling about, looking for trouble. If my suspicions were right, Mr. Branikov would feed and I would be there!

Mr. Branikov departed the stadium from the back entrance. It was dark and quiet, leading down the back alleyway of the high school. I followed at a distance. I thought we were alone.

"Hey, Michael…or is it Michelle? No wait! Wasn't it Jenna?" I heard from behind me, along with sudden laughter.

I turned. It was James Day and his pack, some of the popular boys who I found to be very irritating.

"Come on, James. It doesn't even know what it is," another boy said, as they all laughed again.

The pack walked closer to me. James looked at me and shook his head. "Well, it got rid of its boobs. Maybe we should see if it has any balls."

My anger rose and I saw the vein in James' neck pulsate. He was a jerk. I was losing my thoughts. Everything was starting to spin. *Attack!*

In the blur of the moment, out of the darkness, I felt a hand on my shoulder.

"Not now. It's okay," a calming voice whispered in my ear.

I turned to find Mr. Branikov behind me. I heard the pack of boys scatter. Mr. Branikov was standing there. He smiled, pushed the hair away from my eyes and gently said, "Walk with me."

I learned that night that Mr. Branikov was who I'd thought him to be. However, he had not doomed me to this life but had saved me. I learned that while I had still been Jenna, before I had come forward about my true self, I had been very unhappy. Mr. Branikov told me that he'd found me below the old town bridge with hardly a breath left. He'd chosen to save me.

I didn't remember any of this. It was after this moment that I had gone forward in my life. I'd found my new self. I found new meaning. I'm a new creature—actually two new creatures—although I think I've always been the one. I've found happiness at last.

Chapter Two

Deciphering the Miscreants from the Blameless

Mr. Branikov showed me more that night.

"Those boys were not immoral, Michael. They were wrong in the way they treated you, yes, but they are still young. They are still learning. Like you, they deserve a chance at life. Don't you think, Michael?"

I looked at this man. He was not my history teacher of old — now he was something new, a teacher of my new reality. We stood facing each other in the *dark* alleyway. His eyes were piercing my soul. I could feel his inner thoughts mixing with my own.

"Yes, Michael, we are now connected," he said as he could see me staring into his eyes. "and no, we are not soulless creatures. Come. Tonight, lesson one."

This man, now someone totally different than I'd expected and still mysterious, led me the back way into lower downtown. We took the unseen path, staying in the shadows, the lonely way. Through the unlit and dreggy alleyways where no one else dared venture except maybe a weary alley cat or two, we crept.

Mr. Branikov led me into a part of town that I had never wandered into alone. The place was filled with those in town who everybody turned a blind eye to — the ladies of the night, drug lords, those seeking drugs, violent humans and the lost souls with no other place to go. It was that place every town had but every town denied.

I moved my steps closer to Mr. Branikov. Even though I wasn't sure of him yet, he still felt safer than what was now around me. I felt his hand on my shoulder. He must have sensed my unease.

"It's okay, Michael. We are safe. It is those around us who perhaps are not." Mr. Branikov gave me a little grin.

He was right. *What am I afraid of?* I knew that I had found some new strength of late, some tremendous strength. I thought maybe it was the T, my new hormone drugs changing my body, but now that I thought it over… *This new strength, is…well, unhuman-like.*

Mr. Branikov looked at me and chuckled. "You know, Michael, it's not just strength that you have gained. There are many more powers that come with this new gift."

"Wow! Yeah, like mind reading?"

Mr. Branikov smiled. "Yes, to a degree, like mind reading — maybe more like sensing what someone is thinking. And, Michael, being able to control what someone else thinks as well."

I furrowed my brow. "Really?"

He just chuckled. "Shush! Listen to your thoughts. Listen to *their* thoughts." He pointed across the street.

We were still tucked away in the darkness of the alley. A group of apparent miscreants stood under the rays of a streetlight, kitty-corner and across the street, just within our view.

Mr. Branikov stood quietly with his eyes closed, perhaps listening to the thoughts of the one who would become our victim. I followed his lead. I shut my eyes. I could hear him in my mind.

"Venture your mind out, find the group of voices," he said.

I heeded his instructions. Voices filled my inner thoughts.

"I need more. I need some smack."

"Skank, leave me alone tonight. I'm so tired of you."

"Let's do something different for a change."

"Money, money, let's nick the place across the street. Forget these guys. I'll get all the money for myself."

"I'm tired. I am just so tired."

I could hear the chatter from the corner. It wasn't the same thing that I was sensing in their thoughts. This I found very intriguing.

"Now what?" I whispered.

"We wait. We want the thief. He is more wicked than I think you sensed. I felt more from his past. Secondly, never do a druggy…bad side effects. If you can rid the town of a drug dealer, if he is clean, then do so, because then everyone is better off. Agree?" Mr. Branikov gave me a most serious look.

I nodded.

He continued, "Don't do drunks, unless you're desperate. Now, there is one in this group that still has hope in their soul. Leave that one be."

"Um, got it," I replied, nodding again, for I indeed understood and felt the emotions from my new teacher as well.

Time passed slowly. I stood there, trying to be patient. Waiting. My urges were becoming hard to resist. I could feel my bloodthirst driving me to attack. These unknown beings stood helplessly only a short distance from my reach.

The streetlight began to blur. I took a step forward, but I felt a strong hand across my chest. Something held me back.

"*Control... Control, Michael,*" he said within my thoughts.

I broke out of my trance. I found Mr. Branikov smiling at me.

"Soon... Be patient."

I nodded, but still I sighed. It was hard for a young, hormonal, new-teen boy, who was also a new creature, to be patient. He was asking a lot, but I waited.

Finally, after what felt like hours but were probably only minutes, the group of miscreants went their separate ways. It was time! Time to fill my need, my thirst.

The human that had thoughts of money did indeed hang around on the corner. Yes, he planned further. When his friends were gone, he was going to break into the pawn shop and steal whatever he could manage — a dash and run, before the cops got there, knowing the alarm would sound as he smashed a window. It was a simple plan from a simple-minded, lowlife scum. He would likely have gotten away with it — that was, if we hadn't been there. *Not tonight.* Tonight would be his last evil deed.

We attacked. More like, Mr. Branikov attacked before the shop's window was smashed, before any alarm would sound. The evil-doer was dragged into the alleyway and choked unconscious before I even knew what had happened.

Dang, don't mess with Mr. Branikov. He's stronger than he appears. Stronger than I would have ever imagined.

He smiled at me as he carried the unconscious body farther into the alley, deeper into the darkness of the night. I followed him and watched as he dropped the body into the sludgy mud, hidden now behind a building's storage shed.

I walked up to the man's head. Though unconscious, he was still alive. The neck vein of the victim pulsated. Mr. Branikov looked at me, smiled, then we filled our ravening thirst.

A misty fog rolled in, almost in perfect timing, like Mr. Branikov had known it would come. We carried the body, now drained of blood and lifeless. We gave this lowlife scum no second thought, for we both were rejuvenated, high on life, and we had rid the town of one more criminal, one more human that everyone would be better off without.

The fog continued to fill the air, like a heavy, white-wool blanket. It was easy to carry the body through the town streets without being seen. I think Mr. Branikov could have easily carried the body alone, as perhaps now I could have, but we both shared the load, as a team of two.

We found our way to the forest that sat at the town's edge. Deep within it we ventured, farther into the forest than I had ever wandered. It was thick and overgrown with lots of creatures about, tough enough to negotiate without having a cumbersome body to carry. It was also easy to get lost, hurt or who knew what else. *Who am I kidding? I am lost. I sure hope Mr. Branikov knows how to get out of here.*

I heard him chuckle. *"Just stay with me,"* entered my mind.

Dang, I better not think ill of the man. This could be tricky.

Mr. Branikov chuckled again. "That's right. Keep your thoughts, well…hmm, I guess your next lesson might be on how to control your thoughts and how to control the thoughts of others too. By the way, when it is just us, please call me Drakon."

"Yes!" I replied. *I so want to learn about my new powers.* He just laughed. I had so many questions about my new life. I had so many questions about both of my new lives, actually. Things were so confusing right now.

"Wow, you do have a lot going on, Michael. We will sort it all out. Patience," Drakon said with a reconfirming grin.

I smiled. It was nice to have someone to reassure me on all issues.

Finally, we came to a stop.

"Here," Drakon pointed.

There was a rocky outcropping. Limestone, I guessed, overgrown with ferns, moss and whatever else grew in this wet, overgrown, dark and murky forest.

Drakon took the body the rest of the way, thrown over his shoulder. He heaved it up a few rocks then over and down into a rocky crevasse. I didn't even hear the lifeless body hit bottom. Gone. Maybe joining others… I didn't know, nor did I care to find out. It was another human that the cops wouldn't bother to search for, vanished forever.

Chapter Three

Unanswered Questions

We went our separate ways. There went another blue shirt, adorned in blood and gone from my wardrobe. I was going to need to buy more T-shirts at this pace. I had been soaking them in hydrogen peroxide to get the blood out and adding a little bleach. The shirts were perhaps looking like something from the 1960s and not something I could be seen wearing to school these days, not unless I enjoyed getting made fun of, which I didn't. I didn't need any help in that department. I already got laughed at enough as it was.

Into the garbage another shirt would go, tucked away where Mom or Dad would not see the hideous thing as the trash got taken away. I would volunteer to take out the garbage. Oh, what a good kid I was — or so my parents thought.

I think Mom knew something was up, but she didn't ask questions. I think she was worried that it had to do with bullying at school and the choice of my new transition of F2M. She would only ask if I was okay. Of course, I would always tell her yes.

The good thing was that Mom always gave me money to resupply my shirts. It wasn't that I liked anything expensive anyway. I just wanted a good, soft, old-fashioned blue-shaded T-shirt of some sort—or a blue hoodie would suffice. I was learning, though, that I should not wear my favs out on those particular evenings. Maybe a red shirt would be smarter. I peered into my closest that next morning before school. *Hmm, everything seems to be a shade of blue. Geez, like my whole closet, nothing but blue.* I chuckled. *Maybe I should widen my horizons a bit.*

I donned what else but my blue jeans and a blue T-shirt. I took one last look in the mirror before heading out of the door. I did like the way my new body was starting to form. The T was doing a good job. I could look into the mirror and it actually looked like me.

Mom smiled at me as she forced me to grab a blueberry muffin to eat on my way to school. *Arrgh, moms… I guess they do love us, no matter what.* I knew that my mom had been through a lot. I felt bad for her sometimes. I wasn't the only one getting harassed for my new change. I knew she had been catching plenty of flack too. Even Aunt Jeanine, Mom's sister, was giving her crap. I knew that they had been going round and round about me. I had overheard plenty of their conversations. Aunt Jeanine didn't get it. She meant well and was truly worried about me, but she just didn't understand.

I gave Mom a kiss on the cheek and was out of the door. I met up with Callie in the school's front courtyard before the first bell. Callie was my oldest and best friend. I could always count on her for everything. She even understood the F2M transition that I was making. When I'd first told her, she'd just said, *'Geez, dude, what took you like so long to figure that out?'* I think she'd known since we had been in elementary school.

I told Callie almost everything. However, I was keeping one secret from her — this other change, this bloodthirst. That fact, I would keep to myself for now.

"Bro, you were supposed to show up early today, so we could compare our American history notes," Callie said as I walked up.

Oops… Oh, man, I forgot. Dang, with everything going on, how do I tell Callie that history is like the last thing on my mind?

"Oh, geez. Dang, girl, I forgot. Sorry." I plastered a pleading look for forgiveness on my face.

Callie shook her head at me, tossing her twisted black braids and beads from side to side and rolling her eyes. "What is up with you lately? You've been as bad as my grandpa about remembering things, I swear."

I looked at her with a frown then — what else could I do? I laughed.

"What? Geez, thanks a lot."

Luckily, Jonathan came waltzing in to save me, almost skipping around the corner and looking happy as a lark. Right between the two of us, he stopped.

Everyone thought Jonathan was Q for sure, but I didn't really know, nor did I give a rat's ass. I mean, look at me. I knew he did not want to become a girl. It wasn't like it was a transgender issue, but he was for sure pretty feminine — or at least I thought so. He had never had a girlfriend and he didn't ever really talk about such things, so I had always just left it alone. So really, who knew? Who cared? He was a true friend and one who didn't judge me, so I would always try to return the favor. Still, though, he made me laugh.

"Jonathan, why so glum?" Callie joked.

Jonathan looked at us both and put his arms around us as we walked toward the front doors of the school building. "Somebody likes me," he said to a musical tune.

"Who?" Callie immediately questioned.

"Hmm-m," Jonathan bantered back.

I was chuckling. "Is it Nash? The smart kid from chemistry class?" I asked.

Jonathan stopped us in his tracks. He looked astonished. "What?" he exclaimed. "No, you dork. It's not a dude!"

What? See? You shouldn't judge people. All these years of thinking just maybe Jonathan was gay, then what? He up and finds himself a woman. Ha! Who knew?

"Oh?" I replied with a smirk, a raised eyebrow and a little question to my tone.

Callie gave me a scowl.

I caved. "Come on, bro. Who? Tell us who?" I begged.

Drrriiinnngg! The first class bell rang.

"Later." Jonathan jogged off, turned and gave Callie and me a big, ornery grin.

Jonathan had ruined my concentration. All I could think about during my morning classes was, *Who is it Jonathan is hooked up with?* The brat. Every time I saw him in the hall between classes, I would ask him and he would just smile and shrug.

"Arrgh!" I grumbled out of frustration

Fourth period came around, the last class before lunch. I happened by Mr. Branikov. He must have been rummaging through my thoughts. He chuckled as I walked past him. I turned to get a second glance. He pointed to his forehead and mouthed, "Practice."

Oh yeah, you dork. I have these new powers. I will find Jonathan's new love. I can search his mind.

I met up with Jonathan and Callie for lunch. It was time. I would venture out and experiment with my new ability. *I don't know... Is it a sacred thing? Should I probe the mind of my friend? Yeah. This will be good practice.*

I could hear Callie babbling on about something in the background. I pretended to listen, but I wasn't. I was concentrating on Jonathan's mind. It was not something to behold. Of all the things he could be thinking about, he was thinking about my piece of pizza I wasn't eating that was sitting on my plate in front of me.

What a dweeb. I chuckled and slid my plate to my friend. His eyes lit up in wonderment. I nodded, letting him know he could have it.

Come on, Jonathan. Who is your new love?

Jonathan's mind was full of all kinds of nonsense, including how good my pizza was tasting. I finally gave up.

"Jonathan! Who likes you? And obviously you must like them back?" I asked him out of frustration.

He just smiled as he took a big bite of my slice. *A thought in his mind.* Finally, I got him on the proper path.

"Junie!" I blurted out. "Juniper the cheerleader?"

A girl. Whoa! And one of the popular girls at that!

Jonathan choked on his mouth full of pizza. Half of it came flying out, spraying across at Callie and me. "Eww," we moaned as we wiped the food from our arms and wherever else it had landed.

"Dang, Michael! How did you guess?"

I shrugged. "Hmm-m, lucky?"

Who knew? All this time, Jonathan is a wolf in sheep's clothing. This, though, would surely mean trouble. The popular boys—the football players—would not stand for the likes of a guy like Jonathan stealing one of theirs—a popular girl. I feared for my friend. Danger lay ahead for Jonathan. There was no doubt in my mind.

Jonathan filled Callie and me in on the whole story. Evidently he'd had several advanced level classes with Junie over the years. They had even spent a lot of time after school, studying together. They had become close friends, secret friends. No one had been the wiser.

Finally, it was Junie who'd had enough. She'd decided that she didn't care what others thought anymore. Her affections had grown for Jonathan over the years. She wanted to be with him and nothing was going to stop her. Junie had decided to display her feelings toward Jonathan to the entire school. Of course, Jonathan had been delighted and hadn't argued at all, even though his life might now be at risk.

Jonathan was beside himself. I don't think he ever had a girl like him that way. It was glorious to see him and all his joy. I dared not ruin it for him, even though in the back of my mind, I feared gravely for his physical wellbeing.

What will I do? I decided simply to watch over my friend, to keep a close eye on him at all costs. He was going to need my help, I feared.

That night I tossed and turned. My bed sheets — and my gut — were twisted into a knot by morning. I had enough on my mind. Now my friend had added to my already-full plate.

Jonathan's life with this new girlfriend did start me wondering. It came to my attention that my own love life had been lacking. Void. As a matter of fact, with all my own issues, I had never had a chance to ponder what a life with someone else might be like. Heck, I didn't even know. *Do I like girls? Do I like boys? Wow, have I ever crossed paths with a soulmate yet? How will I know?* These questions filled my mind. By the time I had gotten myself dressed for school, I'd decided it was time to move forward with my life. I had my friends, but maybe it was time for something more. *Oh geez, I hope I don't fall in love then bite them to death. Kill them in a blood-thirst rage! Oh man.* Now *that* was something else to think about.

Out of the door and off to school. Thank goodness for Mom's loving smile and the blueberry muffin she made me take on my way out. There was nothing better to calm my mind.

By that morning, the entire school already knew about Junie and Jonathan. Like I expected, the popular kids were not happy. The geeks and nerds were elated!

I would watch Jonathan as much as I could between classes. At lunchtime, he would be most vulnerable. However, I also needed to talk to Mr. Branikov. I had my own problems to deal with. I had questions. *But how? When?*

Third period, I sensed something in my mind. It was him!

Dang, how does he do that? How does he know? I haven't even been close to him today.

"Come see me. Fourth period. I have Study Hall. Get a hall pass." His thoughts came clearly into my mind.

That was easy for him to ask. *How do I get a pass?* That was the question.

I would pull the old 'I am having a medical issue.' I didn't use it much. I was overall a good student, so I knew my teacher wouldn't question it. Also, my fourth period teacher was kind of an old-fashioned guy. He wouldn't want to question me on any of my transgender issues that I might be going through. I was pretty sure of that.

Hall pass in hand…no problem. I knocked on Mr. Branikov's classroom door. Yes, at school, he would still be Mr. Branikov. It would be too strange to call him Drakon in a place such as this. Dang if he wasn't already opening the door by my second tap. He knew I was there. Psycho…or, I supposed, psychic.

He held the door open and motioned for me to come into the classroom. *But there are other kids in here?* He pointed to an empty desk. A few of the students looked up and gave me a puzzled stare, but most of the students were busy, trying to get their homework done so they didn't have to take it home.

"Back to work," Mr. Branikov whispered to the few students whose attention had strayed. I set my books down. Luckily, I still had the book from my last class in my hand. I laid them out in front of me. *This is confusing. I didn't come here to study. I have questions!*

"Yes. I know you do. I am ready to answer." He was in my mind again. *"Besides, you need to practice this skill."*

I looked up at Mr. Branikov. He was sitting behind his desk, looking at a book like nothing was going on. This was intriguing. Something new. A discussion of the minds. *What the heck? Why not?* I was game. Plus, I wanted answers!

Okay, typical vampire stuff first. I concentrated on a thought. *"At some point, is the sunlight going to turn me to dust?"*

I watched Mr. Branikov's face. A small grin formed. I waited for his answer to enter my thoughts.

I found out that it was a myth. I would *not* turn to dust. However, because my vision was greatly improved, like a panther in the dark, bright sunlight could be hard on my heightened vision. I was enlightened to the fact by my new mentor that I likely should get a good pair of sunglasses.

Second question…garlic. *"Am I going to all of a sudden have an adverse or deadly reaction to garlic?"*

"That's funny. My ancestor, Vlad Tepes, just didn't like garlic. I, however, quite like it myself."

I chuckled and awkwardly broke the silence in the room. The kids sitting next to me gave me a strange glare. *Oh yeah, I have to remember this is an unheard conversation.* I looked to Mr. Branikov. He gave me a raised eyebrow then went back to his book.

"*Okay, next question. How about a stake through the heart? Will that kill me?*" I sent my question into his thoughts.

I could sense his silent laughter. That must be what he meant by 'sensing things'. "*Well now, a stake through the heart. That would kill anybody, wouldn't it?*"

After going over all the vampire myths and finding that they were all that, just myths, a bunch of crap, I finally had an important question, one of love. "*Would I kill one that I love in a bloodthirsty rage?*"

There was silence. Then finally an answer arrived, sort of. "*Michael, have you killed anyone that you have loved yet?*"

That was easy. *Of course not!* I guess I didn't need Mr. Branikov for that one. I already knew the answer. I just had to look for it. I knew that I wouldn't kill anybody that I truly loved. *Easy.*

Drrriiinnnggg! Fourth period had ended. Time had gone by too quickly. I smiled at Mr. Branikov as I gathered my books from the desk. As I walked out of the door, I heard yet another thought. "*Michael, your question that you did not ask... Don't go looking for love. It will find you soon enough – when the time is right and with the right person. You will know.*" I heard him chuckle. "*Usually when you don't expect love, that's when it shows up.*"

I turned at the doorway and gave my mentor a little smile and a nod, then I was off to lunch. *Oh, yes.* Change of thoughts in an instant. *Protection!* I had to protect Jonathan. Lunch would bring danger. I could sense it.

Chapter Four

Football Players for Lunch

I made Jonathan and Callie sit at the last table in the lunchroom. At least that way I only had to watch in one direction, forward. I hoped the danger would come from in front of us.

My friends wondered why we were sitting somewhere different than our normal table, but they decided to appease me after only a bit of grief.

"Really? You have to ask?" I looked at Callie and gave her an eye roll with an added side glance to Jonathan. She got it. Jonathan however, as smart as he was at school, didn't have any common sense. He was clueless. Sometimes I wondered how these smart people made it through life.

I was lucky enough to get down my fries before the trouble began. As I expected, the football players had formed a small squad, and they were now approaching us. I was paying close attention. Jonathan and Callie were oblivious.

James Day, who was not actually a football player but a basketball player, and thus noted as a jock, was definitely one of the popular boys, if not the leader of them all. He was the boy I'd almost attacked in the alley behind the school after the football game. His squad comprised all the popular football players, all the brutes.

My adrenaline rose as the bullies came nearer. James' neck was pulsating as he tossed a football up and down in his hand. *Calm yourself, Michael. Stay calm.* I took a few deep breaths. That was when Callie and Jonathan finally noticed the approaching trouble-makers.

Zzzziippp! James threw the ball at a high speed right toward Jonathan's head. Without even a thought, I reached out and grabbed it out of the air. My own mouth fell open. *Obviously a new power. Super reflexes!* Callie's brown eyes were open about as big as they could get. I gave her an 'I don't know' look and a shrug.

James and the football players had all stopped in their tracks. They were as shocked as my friends and I were. This all from a guy they had never seen in phys ed or sports, someone who they did nothing but ridicule. It was a pretty amazing catch.

"Toss it back!"

I looked at the miscreants. I laughed. I had no idea what I was doing, but before I knew it, I had placed the ball between my hands. *Kapoofff!* The football deflated. It was no more. Only a brown piece of leather remained, now worthless.

I tossed the leather back to James.

"Oops." I laughed.

The hornets' nest had been stirred. There was no doubt that they were going to attack. I stood up to meet the challenge, not knowing what my new abilities would bring.

"Stop!" a female voice screamed from the ever-growing crowd. It was Junie.

Dang it! She's going to ruin my fun.

Junie marched in among us and stood right between James and me. She was indeed feisty. Jonathan was going to have his hands full with this one.

"Stand down, James!"

James looked at Junie, gave a big sigh, turned and looked at his mob. "Come on, guys. Let's go. It ain't worth it."

Wow. I don't know what Junie had over James, but whatever it was, it was powerful.

I could hear the group of boys, mumbling and grumbling as they walked away. They were also passing around the deflated football. That was going to give them something to think about for a while. Actually, knowing those dorks, they were probably going to see if any of them could do the same thing. I would have liked to be a fly on the wall of the football locker room later that day. I was sure it would have been quite the show, especially when none of them could explode a football between their hands. That would make them wonder about me. Maybe that would give Jonathan a break for a bit. We'd see.

Junie joined us for the rest of the lunch hour. It was funny seeing Jonathan so into someone. He was like a slave to her every need. Geez, he would never in a million years treat Callie or me so nice. It was hilarious.

Surprisingly, I liked Junie, even though she was a popular girl. She was smart and funny. She seemed to fit right in with our little group. The cool thing was that she didn't care what anybody else thought as she sat there with us at lunch. *Hmm, most popular kids wouldn't sit within a stone's throw of our table.*

A couple of other geeky kids joined us—Liam and Shelly. I think they did so just so they could say they'd sat with Junie. She didn't care. Neither did we. There was no harm. It was just good and fun for everyone, and Jonathan? Well, he was as happy as I had ever seen him. No way would I let anyone ruin that.

Chapter Five

Shanty Town

I didn't hear any more from the popular group of boys that day, but I suspected that they would be back soon enough. Callie was off to the library after school. Jonathan was off with Junie for some AP chemistry studying. Obviously, that wasn't for me. I would put my schoolwork off until after supper, like I did most days. My mind needed a break. I had my routine.

Off to the gym. It was down the road from our house, about two miles — a good run for me. I took the back roads, different routes when I could, and enjoyed my run. Then I would hit the weights at the gym. It was important to me. I was on the T for a reason. I wanted a new body, one that I felt good in. Well, part of that was up to me, so I worked out hard in the gym, unbeknownst to those popular boys, those jocks at school.

Now, though, as I jogged down a dirt road that ran along some country fields, I wondered, *Have I been lifting enough weights? I am obviously stronger now, but is it my trans — or is it that other new change?*

I noticed, as I jogged past an old, shabby part of town, that my bloodthirst was starting to come around again. I was ravenous. It left me craving. I tried to block it from my mind.

As I jogged, I looked across the railroad tracks. The houses were just shacks and shanties. *Who lives there? Are they criminals? Perhaps there's someone who I could fill my thirst on, but what if they are just people who are down on their luck?*

A big, beastly dog came out of nowhere on a mad dash and startled the bejesus out of me. I sensed that I was going to become this dog's playful prey. *Oh crap!* I picked up my pace, still keeping a watchful eye on the beast.

Craassh! Kathud! I ran somebody over smack dab in the middle of the usually and supposedly quiet road. Down they went.

The dog had stopped. It was possibly a bit scared too but still barking like a raging animal. A large and noisy flock of birds abruptly flew up from the nearby tree and a little girl stood and screamed.

My mind swirled in confusion. In a moment's time, I caught my bearings. At my feet, a girl sat on the dirt road. She had messy hair and grungy clothes. I couldn't tell if the filth on her face was from her falling into the dirt road or if it was a more permanent fixture. Her eyes were sad, somehow.

We just stared at each other for a moment. Then she finally broke the silence. "Really? Dude... Don't you watch where you're going when you're running?"

She seemed unhurt. I looked down at her and smiled then held out my hand to give her a little help. She grumbled, denied my hand and pushed herself up. She dusted off the dirt from her pants, although I wondered if I would be able to tell any difference.

"I don't think we've met before?" I asked. Somehow this girl seemed a bit familiar.

The younger girl, who looked about five or six and who had been screaming earlier, took the older girl's hand and tried to pull her down the road. "Come on, Haddie. Let's go."

The older girl resisted, turned to the younger one and whispered, "Just a minute."

"I'm Hadley...like you would know if you paid attention at school." She huffed and shook her head at me in disgust.

Crap. I knew I should have known her. "You all right?" I asked, but really I was trying to probe her mind for more information and failing disastrously.

"Yeah, whatever. I'm fine."

The two girls started off down the road, Hadley holding on to the younger one's hand. I chose to walk along beside the girls. I wasn't sure what to say, but for some reason I wanted to know more about this Hadley. I was intrigued.

"You live over there?" I tilted my head toward the shanties.

A thought entered my head. This girl, Hadley, was sitting in a classroom at the back — alone, quiet, sad. I did know her — or know of her. Many pictures of her were in my mind now — her at school, always alone, always distant.

"Does it matter if I live over there?" she replied with an irritated voice.

I shrugged. "Um, no, not really. I was just asking."

"Where were you headed anyway?"

I chuckled a little. "Um, I'm on my way to the gym." I gave a little flex of my bicep for some reason unknown to me. I don't know what possessed me to do that, like that was supposed to be impressive or something.

Hadley laughed. Really laughed. *Now come on, I don't think it's that bad.*

"You're kind of funny. I've seen you at school too. You're different."

Now what in the world did she mean by that? I could construe that statement to mean many different things. Did she mean my F2M changes? Did she mean my demeanor was different? Had she seen other changes, the secret thing?

I didn't know what to say, so I just gave her my name. "I'm Michael."

She laughed again. "Yeah, like I know that already."

After I got my moronic antics out of the way, we had a normal conversation. Well, somewhat normal. I found out that Hadley did indeed live in one of the shanties. Evidently her father had fallen on hard times, lost his job and had not been able to find employment in more than a year. To further this poor girl's story, her mother had passed away from ovarian cancer only two years before. Hadley was now left to care for her younger sister Lily, while her father fell deeper and deeper into depression and despair.

We came to the end of the dirt road. I needed to head on to the gym. I yearned to stay. I wanted to hear more about Hadley. She was a strange girl, but I did have my routine to tend to. I had to get on with things.

"Um, I turn here." I pointed down the street toward the gym.

Lily was pulling Hadley's hand in the opposite direction, back to the shanties. She obviously wanted to go home.

"Later. Maybe see you tomorrow at school." Hadley smiled and gave me a wave.

"Yeah, sure. See ya around." I took off on my run again, faster this time, trying to be impressive.

Meeting this new girl put a dilemma into my new plan. Shanty-town could no longer be on my list of possible new feeding grounds. I would have to venture out. As a matter of fact, I'd go out tonight!

Chapter Six

Drakon Branikov

I had a nice dinner with Mom and Dad, accompanied by the usual discussion—Dad's work, my school and friends and Mom's day. Nothing new. Although I did tell them about meeting a new friend, but they really didn't pay attention. It was all just pointless talk.

"Oh yes, that's nice, dear," Mom said as she cleared off the dinner plates. I smiled, got up and gave her a hand. I explained to Mom and Dad that I had loads of homework and would be shut up in my room for the remainder of the night.

"I'll see you guys in the morning."

They both nodded and wished me good evening. They pretty much left me alone. It was nothing out of the ordinary. As long as I was getting good grades and staying out of trouble, they weren't going to interfere.

I did do my homework, then I waited. Time on the clock ticked by like drips off an icicle, irritatingly slow. *Are Mom and Dad ever going to go to bed?*

Finally, the light down the hall switched off. It was time. I would sneak out. My thirst was intense. Things were blurring together. I felt like a cloudy haze was about to enclose my entire being.

I chose to go out of the window. The hallway creaked too much. Old houses were noisy like that. My second-story bedroom was no problem now. I leapt down like a cat and landed lightly on my feet.

I looked around. There was no one out and about on our street. Only a few lights were on. *Not a problem.* I could sneak through the neighborhood. My new vision would guide me easily through the darkness. I avoided the lighted areas of the streets.

I headed to the same area of town that Mr. Branikov, Drakon, had taken us before — the place of the low-lifes, where the drug lords and skanky ladies hung out.

I quickly navigated the back streets of town. The scenery changed quickly. More garbage was lying around and there was a dank feel to the air. Even the smell of the area was unpleasant. It didn't take me long to find an evil-doer.

He was standing under the streetlight on a corner in that wretched neighborhood. In the alleyway, I stood back, staying under the cover of darkness. I studied the man and concentrated on his thoughts.

He was a drug dealer. Not a user, though. He was one to take advantage of the weaker minded, the addicts below him. He would get the weak addicted to his drugs then take them for every last penny they had.

Yes, this will be my target. Evil, yet clean blood.

I needed to coax him away from the light, into the darkness of the alley. There I would quench my thirst.

I waited until no one seemed to be around. I stepped forward onto the lighted sidewalk. "Hey, I have money," I hollered as I waved my wallet around. I beckoned for the man to come to me, then I stepped back into the darkness. *Come this way.* I tried to command him. I was new at this. I didn't know if it would work. Hopefully, the man's greed would be enough to lure him to me.

The evil drug dealer couldn't resist, and it really didn't matter now.

"Where did you go?" the drug dealer asked as he stepped deeper into the alley.

"Here." I lured him farther.

"You looking for something good, kid?"

"Oh, yes…and I got loads of money." I held out my wallet.

The man laughed. "You have to be the dumbest kid ever. What's to keep me from just taking your money? Look around you, kid. It seems that it's just the two of us."

I chuckled. "Indeed." I pounced. It was a tremendous feeling. I felt the haze lift. I was strong, revived. It was like everything was good in the world again. It was a wondrous feeling, even at this man's death. I cared not.

However, my bliss was soon ruined. A car suddenly turned into the alley. In my rush, I hadn't paid attention to the sounds on the street. *Idiot.* The headlights blinded me. The car's front bumper stopped a few feet from my murderous scene. I looked toward the car, the blood trickling down my chin. Staring down at my shirt in the lights, it was almost mystical in appearance. Once again, my blue-shaded shirt was adorned in blood. However, it was one more shirt that would be unwearable.

I heard one car door slam then a second. *No more.*

"What the hell? Is it Ray? This kid killed Ray!" a man's voice screamed from behind the blinding headlights.

"What's he doing?" another man's voice hollered.

"Oh hell!" one of the men screamed.

I jumped up, finally out of the blinding lights. Two men were staring at me, dumbfounded by the gruesome sight of their friend — or maybe their boss — who was now dead. There was blood everywhere.

The man on the passenger side quickly pulled out a gun. "Demon! Stay back!"

My adrenaline rushed through my body. The new blood pulsated through my veins. Before I even knew what I was doing, I was at the man's side. I had the man's gun hand held in my own. We struggled. With defiant force, I pushed his arm toward his friend. *Bang!* The gun went off. He'd shot his own friend while trying to shoot me.

The struggle continued. *Bang.* A nick to my side. A burning sensation along my left flank. I ignored the pain, couldn't give it a thought right now. *His life or mine?* I forced the man's hand down and toward his own body. *Do it! Do it!* I concentrated. *Bang!* He pulled the trigger.

The man collapsed to the ground, gasping for air then silent a moment later. I walked over to the first man who'd been shot. *Dead.* This was a disaster! One dead, I'd needed, I'd planned for, but now three were dead at my hands. Most likely all were evil-doers, scum-dogs, but that was still not what I'd expected to happen.

The gunshots would have been heard. I had to act fast. I was panicked. *Crap! Crap! Shit!* My mind raced, with no good ideas coming to me.

I looked down at my side. Blood was oozing out of a significant gash and dripping down onto the waistline of my jeans. However, it only seemed to be the outer flesh, the tissue of my oblique muscle. Still, it burned, hurt and was making a mess.

I wasn't paying attention once again so I was startled by a hand on my shoulder. *Oh Jesus!* I jumped, yet in an instant I knew that it was okay. It was Mr. Branikov. It was Drakon. He must have sensed my catastrophic acts.

"Wow! Make a mess of things, did we?"

"Aaahh," I gave out a deep sigh of agony at my mess and at the same time a sigh of relief that Drakon was there. "It got a little out of hand."

"Yeah, I'd say so. Come on. We have to be quick."

I didn't have a clue what to do or where to start. I started to pick up the man at my feet, the one who I'd forced to shoot himself.

"No, leave them. No time. Besides, it appears as a drug deal gone bad with those two. This one, however, we have to get rid of — and quickly." Drakon pointed to my first victim, the *intended* victim.

Before I could do anything, Drakon had the body over his shoulder. The way he lifted the lifeless corpse, one would have thought it was only a mannequin, like it had no weight at all. "This way!"

I followed Drakon. We took the back way out of the alley. We left the two gunshot victims where they were. I was sure the scene with all the blood would be confusing for the police, but once again, would they really care? More thugs and drug dealers dead.

We rushed through the darkness of the night. There was no forest in this direction. We couldn't backtrack.

The police would surely be all over that part of town by now. I was worried.

Drakon must have sensed my concern. His thoughts entered my mind. *"It's okay. I have a place."*

As we ducked in and out of dank and dark alleyways, Drakon lectured me about my hunting skills and my carelessness. However, in the end, he did let me know that he too had once been new at this and that he had made many mistakes along the way.

He got me thinking. *Did I ever ask Drakon about his story?* What was it? So, I did.

Mr. Drakon Branikov had been born in 1493. *Dang, that makes him how old?* He chuckled as I tried to do the math in my head while he was telling me. His family was from Romania. He told me that his original family name was Tepes, but that they had changed it over the years for protective reasons.

I asked him if the name Drakon stood for Dracula — like everyone has heard about. He laughed and explained to me that his name was an old name and that it was more related to 'dragon'.

He told me his story of being turned, not out of horror, but for reasons much like my own — to save his young life. He'd been dying from a plague. A man named Vlad had come to like him and decided to save him from uncertain death. They were not evil, vicious beings as the myths portrayed them to be, but instead they had become hunted in that time because of fear. The group they had grown to be had finally been forced to split up and flee to different parts of Europe, hiding in secret.

I interrupted his story. "But how did your father become — well, you know — one of these beings in the first place?"

"I wondered when you would ask about that. Curiosity, I know, is hard to resist. My father was not turned by a bat bite like so many movies portray." Drakon went on to explain that Vlad had taken an arduous journey to Constantinople. He'd been trying to thwart the Muslim attacks on Romania by convincing the sultan to be allies rather than enemies, which in the end had proved pointless. He'd travelled to the distant land to negotiate peace for all of their people, for everyone's livelihood. Although, in the end, the people had not appreciated what he'd done and had turned on him.

While in Constantinople, Vlad had been unfortunately bitten by a Black Viper. By some miracle, it didn't kill him. However, this serpent—a serpent of Hell—had carried a virus, a sickness. While most would have died, Vlad had lived, and maybe that had not been meant to be. That had been the start of the ravenous bloodthirst.

Drakon told me that Vlad and his family—or like beings—had always tried to be as moral as they could. Of course, some people would question that. "But a hunter that kills its prey to eat, to survive, is it wrong?" he asked me.

I didn't answer but continued to listen to Drakon's story.

"This is why I choose lost souls, evil souls. Killing is not right. It's only done to survive."

Drakon stopped. I wanted more. He sensed that. He looked over at me, with the body still draped over his shoulder. "We're here."

I had been watching Drakon and following him closely. Listening. Deep in thought. Not paying attention to my surroundings. I looked out.

The town dump! We stood at the edge of the town's dump.

"Yes, you will bury the body deep within that pile. It is due to be plowed over with dirt soon." Drakon answered the question in my thoughts. He pointed to a heaping pile of the town's garbage that was closest to the edge of the dirt canyon, the portion not yet covered.

"Arghh," I groaned. "I will bury the body in this crap?"

Drakon smiled. "Well, it is *your* victim. So yes — and best you bury it deep underneath the trash. We don't want any stray animal digging it out, now do we?"

I shrugged. Dang, he was right. Still, that didn't mean I liked the idea. *Geez, this is going to stink.*

I dragged the body over to the site that we deemed the best area. The good thing about the lifeless body was that it did not leave a trail of blood. The blood was pretty much gone, by my consumption. I dug out heaps of garbage, from old food to poopy baby diapers. I tried not to throw up.

I would definitely have to plan my kills better in the future. That was a good lesson.

With many wretched gags, I finished my task. The body was deep within the pile of garbage and covered completely. I turned and stood there in front of my mentor. I felt as trashy as the garbage I stood upon. I started to step toward Drakon.

"Oh no!" He held out his hand for me to stop. He shook his head.

What? What does Drakon want of me? I knew my clothes were a mess, blood-soaked and now garbage-ridden as well. However, I had no choice. It wasn't like I had any other clothes at hand that I could just magically change into.

"Get rid of the clothes. You must leave them here in the town dump as well." Drakon pointed back to the huge pile of trash that I had just left.

"What?" I exclaimed. Then, I laughed, loudly. He had to be joking. He was not.

"Your clothes cannot be found. They obviously are beyond cleaning." Drakon looked me up and down.

I looked at myself. *Yeah, maybe he has a good point. But what? Go naked?*

Drakon took off his coat. He held it out with one arm and turned his head away so that I was out of his sight.

Oh, I understand now. I stripped down, right there, right in the middle of the town dump, loving the darkness. I shoved my clothes deep into the garbage, hiding them the best I could.

I paused, the moonlight shining down on my naked body. I admired my changed upper body, my new part of me—the part that felt right. Then, I looked farther down. I came to the lower half, still unchanged—a stranger's body to me. Still unwanted, unknown, it felt almost shameful to me.

"Umm-m, Michael!" Drakon got my attention. "We have to get you home, and before the morning light would be nice."

I walked over to Drakon and gently pulled the coat from his hand. I put it on and buttoned it up. I chuckled. It barely covered my nakedness. Thankfully, though, it was better than nothing.

Drakon talked with me a bit about my change on the way home. He had sensed that it was bothering me. He wondered why I had only changed the top half. Why had I stopped there?

I explained to him that Mom and Dad had been so supportive. They, after much counselling, had decided to let me go forward with my F2M change. They were all in. However, it finally came down to a matter of money. They had run out of extra money. While some health insurance plans were getting better about covering some of the gender-dysphoria-related issues, most still fell short. Our family insurance plan covered some cost but also had a large out-of-pocket deductible. Mom and Dad had a limited budget. It wasn't like we were rich or anything.

I told Drakon that I understood. I knew that the testosterone that I took alone cost a lot. I wanted to get a job after school to earn extra money, but Mom wouldn't let me. She told me that I needed to concentrate on my schoolwork and on just being a kid right now. The bottom line was that I would have to wait to complete my change.

Drakon understood and consoled me the best he could. He told me to stay strong and be patient. I thought that was pretty good advice for now.

He said, "You're becoming quite an astounding young man."

I really liked that it made me forget all about the shame that I had felt.

We parted ways. I made it home. Twilight. No morning sun yet, but I knew it was close to peeking out from behind the horizon.

I went to the side of the house. I peered up to my open bedroom window. *Shit! It's a long way up there.* I could climb the tree, drop off onto the roof then scurry over on the ledge to my window. *Oh, that doesn't sound good, especially climbing the tree part with no protective clothes on underneath this coat.* I could go in the front door, but the stair and the hallway would creak for sure. *No, that isn't good either.*

Then, purely by instinct, I did it! I jumped! To my surprise, I reached the lower ledge of my window sill. *Holy crap! Amazing!* I pulled myself in through the window and tried to quietly drop onto the floor. Assuredly, it was probably not as quiet as I would have liked, but as I arose, I didn't hear anyone stirring.

Thank goodness I had been rejuvenated and didn't need much sleep. I had missed this night's sleep for sure. As I stood there in my bedroom, I could smell my own abhorrent stench fill the room with an odor I can't even begin to explain. My own teenage body odor, now that I had extra T, was bad enough, let alone the garbage smells that had adhered to my skin somehow. The Axe deodorant had long worn off. It was enough to make one gag, which I was close to doing.

I needed to get to the shower before Mom and Dad got up. I grabbed my towel that hung off the edge of my bedpost and headed to the bathroom. A hot shower was just what I needed.

As I scrubbed off the blood and scum, I remembered the gunshot. I looked down to my side. There was nothing. No gash, no scar. My wound was healed. I poked, pried and prodded. Nothing. *Amazing! Another cool feature of my new life. Wow! Self-healing. No wonder Drakon looks so good at five hundred twenty-seven years old.* That got me thinking about what his life must have been like, what my life would be like. I was only just beginning.

Chapter Seven

Finding Hadley

I had thrown Drakon's coat in the washer, along with several of my dirty clothes. I did it before Mom was even out of bed that morning. I had to clean Drakon's coat. It would have been too embarrassing to return the thing in such smelly disarray. Plus, it would have stunk up the house. I'm sure Mom would have noticed. It reeked so much!

On another issue...clothes. At this rate, I was going to run out of them. As I said before, Mom gladly gave me extra money to buy some new shirts, but this time I had lost a pair of perfectly good jeans too. Now, those were *not* cheap.

I was going to have to come up with a way to make some coin or find a cheap way to get more clothes. The thrift store entered my mind, but even then I needed additional cash flow. I needed some cool clothes too. I didn't want to be a total outcast. It was bad enough as it was already.

You know, I bet that drug dealer had extra money on him. Dang, I should have checked his pockets before burying him in the dump. Duh, that was stupid.

I had to drag out an older pair of jeans from the bottom of my dresser drawer. *I definitely have to quit wearing my better clothes when I go out on a – well, a hunt.* I thought about it as I sat at the breakfast counter downing some orange juice and a blueberry muffin that Mom had made especially for me. Somehow, the muffin didn't taste quite as good as usual.

As I waited for the clothes dryer to finish, I wondered if I even needed to eat regular food anymore. That was a question I would have to ask Drakon. It could be one of those myths – that our kind don't eat any regular food.

Mom talked with me a bit while having her morning coffee. "Wow, you were sure up early this morning."

"Oh yeah, just needed to wash some of my favs. You know how it is?" I smiled at her and pointed my hand toward the laundry room, causing my blueberry muffin to crumble.

She chuckled. "Oh yes. Heaven forbid you have to wear something else."

"Whatever." I gave her a look, but we both laughed.

I threw my dried clothes in a pile on my bed. They could be put away later...or never. However, I carefully and neatly folded Drakon's coat and tucked it into my backpack. It barely fit. Dang if I didn't have to leave some schoolbooks out. I could easily get through a day without them. No problem.

I wouldn't be able to resist. I'd grab another blueberry muffin on my way out of the door. Not paying attention, I'd been shoveling the muffin into my mouth while walking toward school. *Dang, did I even taste the thing?* There were so many thoughts going through my mind that I found myself at the base of the school's steps before realizing my morning's journey had been completed.

Before classes started, I ducked into Drakon's — now Mr. Branikov since we were back at school — classroom. I left his coat, neatly folded on his desk. I found a piece of paper and quickly scribbled out a simple 'Thank you'.

I hurried out in search of my friends. It wasn't really a search. They were where they always were before school, at the concrete steps just outside the front doors.

Callie, Jonathan and the newest member, Junie, were all sitting on the concrete wall that bordered the steps. Callie laughed at me as I walked up.

"What?" I looked at myself, checking from my shoes to my chest, making sure I had all my clothes fastened up.

"Oh, I don't know, expecting a flood?"

I looked down at my old jeans. They were last year's. *Guess I've grown a bit.* One white sock, one blue sock... I imagine that did stick out a little. Okay, maybe like a neon sign.

"Um, I couldn't find a matching pair." By then all my friends were having a good laugh at my expense.

"Whatever." I shrugged then pushed Jonathan backward off the wall onto the grassy and somewhat-damp lawn.

"Bro! We were just messing with you. You're okay, really." He laughed even harder.

I definitely have to get some new jeans.

I ignored my friends as they continued to talk. I looked around the school yard. I was looking for someone in particular...Hadley.

Found her. She was sitting alone, squatted down by the fence over near the track and soccer fields. She had straggly hair and her clothes were ragged. Although I couldn't judge at the moment, Hadley didn't seem to care about her surroundings. I could tell she was lost in her own world. She was reading a book, deep in thought. I was about to head over to her, but then I was rudely interrupted by a familiar voice.

"Hey, Junie, come with us. You don't want to hang out with these dorks."

I turned to see none other than James and the boys. *Ha, seems they got themselves a new football.* I motioned for them to throw the football our direction, taunting them. I had a most ornery look about me, I'm sure.

"Yeah, right, queer. I don't think so," James said as his little group laughed.

"Not queer," I mumbled.

"What was that? Yeah right, whatever you say, Jenna. Oh, that's right. It's Michael now. Is that it? Is that what you call yourself now?"

"Cut it out, James," Junie said as she shook her head in disgust. "Come on, Michael. These guys aren't worth the trouble."

I turned and looked at Junie, gave her a little smile, then abruptly and surprisingly to everyone, stepped out right in front of James. I had forgotten how much bigger he was than me.

James looked at me and laughed. I, however, stood my ground. I waited. I wouldn't be the first to attack, but I would defend myself. Oh, how I so wanted him to give me a shove. He would discover my wrath.

"Michael!" I turned to see Mr. Branikov standing at the school doors. *Dang it! Busted!* I grabbed my backpack off the concrete wall in a huff, whispered 'later' to my friends and walked away. I ignored the taunts and remarks of the brutish boys in the background.

I met Mr. Branikov, who was wearing a scowl. Before he could mind-probe me with a lecture, I questioned him first with something totally off the subject.

"Do we need to eat real food?"

He looked at me with a puzzled look for a moment then he laughed. He opened up the school doors and gestured that we should walk down the hallway. School was about to start anyway.

"What brings about that question?"

I shrugged. However, I was serious. I did want to know. I looked at him in silence and raised my eyebrows with a sober look on my face. I waited for his answer.

I think once Mr. Branikov figured out that I'd meant what I'd asked, he finally answered. *"Of course, Michael, we eat. You still have to take care of your human body – and, mind you, you will have it for a long time to come, so treat it well."*

"Ahh...okay. *Just wondering,"* I thought back just as the school bell rang.

Drrriiinnngg!

Mr. Branikov shook his head but smiled as I took off down the hallway.

* * * *

Later that morning, I trudged into third period English Lit class. Not paying attention to much of anything, I nonchalantly glanced to the back of the classroom. There she was, sitting quietly and hardly noticeable. All this time, I had never realized that Hadley was in my class.

I walked to the back of the room and plopped my books down on the desk next to hers. She gave me an odd sideways glance.

"Hey. What's up?" I awkwardly asked, mainly because I didn't know what else to say.

"Really?"

I smiled as she gave me no other answer. I slid into the chair beside her. I offered her a Jolly Rancher that I had tucked away in my backpack. Watermelon. I thought about switching it with another, because that flavor did happen to be my favorite. She didn't even pause and swiped it quickly out of my hand. I chuckled. At least I got a little smile back.

We didn't have a chance to talk, but I did manage to write an invite in my notebook, asking her to sit with me and my friends at lunch. She nodded.

I could hardly sit through my next class. My thoughts strayed, all to this Hadley girl. *Who is she really?* It was strange that I had spent all these years in school with this girl and I really didn't know anything about her. Mysterious. She was certainly strange and different, but for some reason she had my attention now.

Drrriiinnngg!

Finally, the lunch bell. I rushed to the lunchroom and grabbed my usual, a couple of slices of pizza and a side salad. Somehow, that felt like it made it healthier, but I was doubtful that it did, especially with all the Ranch dressing that I doused over the lettuce. I was quick to get a table, specifically one with five chairs.

Callie was the first to join me. "Dang, Michael, in a rush today?"

"Sort of… Um, just wanted this table."

Callie gave me a strange look. "Okay. Whatever." Finally, she couldn't stand it and she had to ask, "Why *this* table?"

"Someone is joining us today." I then went on to explain to Callie about Hadley and how I had plowed her over in the middle of the road while out jogging. I told her that I thought she had been going to school with us for a long time and that none of us had seemed to notice her before.

I continued with my story as Jonathan and Junie joined us.

"Oh yeah, I know her. She's that really poor girl," Junie said.

At that moment, the girl herself walked up. It was a bit awkward. We all got really quiet at the same moment. It was obvious that we had been talking about her.

"Uh-hmm-m," Hadley uttered, as she looked at me. I knew she didn't quite know what to do. I quickly pulled out the empty chair to my right, to let her know she should still join us.

"Hello," she barely spoke as she sat with her eyes looking down, too shy to even look at us.

"So what do you want to do for our AP Chemistry experiment?" Junie quickly asked Jonathan, easing the tension.

Junie was pretty smart. She guided the discussion at the table like nothing was different, making our newcomer feel more at ease. As Junie and Jonathan were discussing chemistry matters, which was well beyond my knowledge, I noticed that Hadley didn't have any food in front of her. I didn't want to say anything. I might embarrass her, so I turned to my new ability.

I read Hadley's thoughts. Oh man, she had a lot of things going through her mind. After sorting through many confusing topics, I found what I was searching for. I sensed that she was really uncomfortable sitting here with us, but I also sensed that as she watched us eat, she found herself growing hungry, really hungry. I figured she had no money for lunch.

I had already eaten one of my slices of pizza, so I slid my plate over in front of her, gave her a little nod, stretched and moaned a bit, like I was full already.

"You don't want it?" she whispered.

I shook my head. Her eyes perked up. I could tell she was thankful to have it without even reading her thoughts.

Jonathan saw me slide my plate over. He was used to getting my leftovers. He paused his conversation and gave me a big, glaring stare. I just raised my eyebrows back at him.

"Ouch!"

Junie had kicked Jonathan under the table. Junie obviously understood what was going on. Jonathan however was a little slow on the uptake. *For a smart guy, he sure is stupid sometimes.*

My friends and I enjoyed a nice lunch. We tried to get Hadley involved when we could, but it was tough since we didn't know anything about her. I don't think we overwhelmed her too much. We tried not to ask anything too personal. Overall, I sensed that by the end of lunch, things had gone pretty good. *At least I know she really likes ham and pineapple pizza.*

I was inattentive for the rest of my classes that day. I think even Mr. Branikov had tried to communicate with me, but I'd simply blocked him. I had something else on my mind. *Hey, maybe this is a new skill, blocking out other's thoughts — others like me, that is.* That distracted me for a moment and brought to question, *How many others are there like Mr. Branikov and me?*

I fell into my usual routine after school. I said my usual "Hello, school was great," to Mom, grabbed an apple, threw on my gym clothes and was out of the door.

I headed off on the same route I had taken the last time, down the old dirt road by the shanties. The same dog came out. It was viciously barking, but didn't bite. "Rrrgh," I stopped and growled back. The not-so-vicious dog ran off.

I kept a better eye out down the road this time, hoping to see the girl and her little sister perhaps, but there was nothing, not even a car — just a lonely dirt road.

I slowed to a walk as I came parallel to the shanties. It was humid out today. It was nice that it kept the dust down, but not so nice that I was horribly sweaty. *Dang, if boys don't sweat a lot more than girls.* I had noticed this ever since I had been on the T. I pulled my shirt's underarm pit to my nose. *Not too bad.* At least my deodorant was still working. I would hate to run into the likes of Hadley and smell like one of those boys in the football locker room. *Gross.*

I decided to wander over to the row of shanties, though I was not sure why. It was just an urge. Okay, really, it was the driving curiosity that I had about Hadley.

The place was sad. Some of the houses — if they could be called such — were just sheds, not even having a front door. I could just look right into the people's home. They were shacks of destitution and decay. The smell was mostly unpleasant, that of trash and urine mixed together.

I was starting to feel an overwhelming gloom. However, then I came across at least one nicer shanty, giving me hope. It was more like a small cabin. Someone must have been cooking inside. It smelled of baked bread. This was much better. Hopefully Hadley lived downwind of this place and not in the mix of the earlier places that I had passed by.

I tried peering into the windows as I walked by a few more little shanties, without being too obvious. I didn't want to be creepy or anything.

I came to the seventh one in this nicer area, if that would be appropriate to say. It had a little porch. There was Hadley, sitting on an old, rickety-looking rocking chair. She had a book in her lap, but at the moment she appeared to be laughing at her sister. Lily was sitting below her, playing with a frayed and fairly dirty-looking stuffed unicorn and some sort of princess Barbie doll.

I was standing in front of the porch. It wasn't a high porch. There were only three steps, and the middle one was broken. The shanty behind looked small. *Geez, seems hardly bigger than the shed in our backyard.* I guessed that it had maybe one bedroom. I thought the curtains in the one window were nice. I figured they must have been Hadley's doing.

"What are you doing here?" Hadley was not only surprised at my arrival but also seemed a little bit irritated. *What am I doing here?* "Um…I don't know. What are you up to?" I was such a dork.

After shaking her head, she finally laughed at me. "Well, did you run anybody over on your way here today?"

"No! Geez, no, like only you that one day."

Lily, the cute little sister, gave me an eye roll. *Hmm, never mind. Little monster.*

I looked back up at Hadley. "Want to go to the thrift store?"

Hadley had an astonished look on her face. "I've got no money for such things."

"Well, you don't have to buy anything, but I need some new jeans—and maybe some new shirts. I thought I would check it out. Umm-m, and maybe you could just like come along, you know, for the heck of it."

"You shop at the thrift store?"

"What? Why not? It seems I go through a lot of clothes." I shrugged and gave her a bit of a glare.

She chuckled a little. "Okay. We have to take Lily. Dad's out, so I'm watching her."

"Okay." I shrugged. That was cool by me.

The local thrift store wasn't but a half-mile or so away. It was down on a street that had a few local shops and a couple of restaurants, like a quaint little neighborhood town square.

Lily wasn't too happy about leaving her unicorn and doll behind. I had to promise her some ice cream to keep her from throwing a fit. That seemed to work. Luckily, I had thrown my wallet into my hoodie pocket and it actually had money in it, which wasn't always the case. Mom had given me extra to buy some new shirts, so that would be perfect. The whole thing was not exactly planned, but I thought it was working out quite nicely.

Hadley and I talked as we walked to the thrift store. She told me her dad was supposed to be out looking for work, but she doubted that he was. She guessed that he'd given that up months ago. "More like the local bar is where we would find him."

I wanted to ask her more, like how did she and Lily survive? How did they have any money for food? But I figured I would let her tell me when she was ready.

Hadley asked me, "Why do you run every day?"

I explained to her that I jogged to the gym every day after school. I told her about how I was trying to keep my body fit, that I wanted more muscles. I think she thought that was strange, but she didn't say anything. I sensed it, though. I wanted to tell her about my trans change and why it was important to me, but I didn't know if she was ready for that much personal information yet. I didn't want to scare her off right away.

I could have read her mind, but I was enjoying talking with her, so I didn't. Not right now. Maybe later sometime, if needed.

I found out that Hadley actually liked school, not so much the kids but the classes. I was astonished when she told me she was a straight-A student. I don't know why I was so surprised. *What? Because she is so poor, she can't get good grades?*

She told me that her hope was to someday get out of that place. She would love to go to college, but she didn't know how she could, with her little sister and all. I actually admired her hopes and dreams, but I didn't know what to tell her. I was pretty terrible at that kind of thing. Thank goodness we arrived at our destination.

I opened the door to the Twice Treasures store. Mrs. Day had owned it since...well, since forever — or at least since I had been alive. I thought she was at least a hundred years old, but probably she was more like in her seventies.

"Welcome, kids. Can I help you find anything today?" Mrs. Day greeted us as soon as we entered. I imagined she was bored and would have liked to have just talked with us.

"Um, just looking," I replied.

"Sure. Just let me know if I can help you with anything. I know where everything is in this old store."

I politely nodded and smiled. I could sense Mrs. Day was nothing but a kind old lady. *Dreadful loneliness. Hmm, that's too much. I don't need to sense that much of her inner feelings. Don't want to do that again.*

I shook my head a little to rid the thoughts. "What?" Hadley quietly asked me.

"Oh, nothing. Sorry. Come on. Let's look for some jeans and T-shirts — blue ones, mind you."

Hadley and I found our way to the area with the boys' clothes. Lily gave me a strange look. I had the feeling she was questioning my choice. Young kids are so good at knowing the truth about things. I gave her a glare then reminded her about the ice cream to distract her. I told her we would go right after we were done there. I hoped that would keep her mind busy.

I pulled out a T-shirt from one of the racks. It was simply a plain blue shirt.

"Blah!" Hadley shook her head.

I thought it was nice, and dang, only two bucks, but I put it back on the rack.

"I like blue!" I blurted out.

"Yeah, I got that already. I've seen you at school, ya know."

Plus, what do I have on? Dark blue gym shorts and a light blue hoodie. Duh.

Hadley pulled out a T-shirt. Now it was cool. This shirt was like one of those tie-dyed shirts, but it wasn't just random. It had a pattern. It was mostly blue, with shades of red and purple flowing down from the top.

That will work. Cool, I could get blood on this shirt and dang if no one would be able to tell the difference.

"How much?"

Hadley looked at the tag. "Wow, it's only three bucks. It's a bargain for sure."

"I'll take it!"

We kept searching. Hadley found a couple more shirts, not as cool as the first one but good enough. I found a pair of jeans. After trying them on, I felt they were a pretty good fit, especially for the price. I was beginning to really like this thrift store.

Lily was getting antsy. I figured we'd better cut it short. Three shirts and a pair of jeans — fourteen dollars. I think Mrs. Day gave us a discount.

As I took my bag, a sudden rush of guilt filled my soul. *Maybe I should have offered to buy Hadley something too.* I glanced over to her grungy and tattered clothing. Would it have been offensive, though? Asking to buy her clothing, like I was trying to diss her in some way? I wasn't sure. Maybe next time, once I got to know her better.

I thanked Mrs. Day, then I thanked Hadley for her help too. By this time, Lily was pulling on Hadley's hand, headed toward the exit door. Ice cream it would be.

The diner was a few shops down. It had a counter, much like an old fountain shop, like the one in that old movie, *Back to the Future II*, where all the kids hung out.

A person could sit at the counter on the little round stool that swiveled all the way around. What kid doesn't like that? And ice cream? Anyone could order pretty much any kind of ice cream conglomeration that they could imagine. I thought the simple little sundaes were the best deal — delicious, lots of flavors and most important to me, they were cheap. I liked the hot fudge sundae.

"Yes, give me one of those hot fudge sundaes without the ice cream please," I said to the soda jerk, who was really just the diner's waitress. During the slow hours, she was covering the entire floor. Sometimes, it was one of the high school kids running the soda fountain, but not today.

The waitress looked at me for a moment, then just laughed. Lily and Hadley both looked at me. I knew they weren't sure what would be polite of them to order, since I was paying.

"The sundaes are really good," I said as I gave them both a grin and added a "Yumm!"

Lily gave me a big smile. "I want one of those too...them hot fudge ones," Lily said to the waitress. The waitress looked over to me. I nodded yes, letting her know that it was okay.

Hadley looked over the soda fountain menu forever.

"Ahhh," I sighed.

She gave me a glare.

"Well," I mumbled, Lily giggled.

"Okay, fine. I want a butterscotch sundae, please."

"Oh, good choice. That's my favorite," the waitress said as she took our menus and gave Hadley a reassuring smile. Hadley just smirked, and gave me a 'Ha, so there' look. I should have been annoyed, but I found it funny that I was already getting to know Hadley's looks. It didn't even bother me. I grinned.

We talked more about nothing important, just getting to know each other a little better while enjoying our sundaes.

Lily interrupted us. "I think we should do this every day," she said as she scraped out every last bit of ice cream in her dish.

I chuckled at Lily and smiled at Hadley. Hadley patted her little sister on the head. "Wouldn't that be nice, Sis? Wouldn't that be nice?"

Hadley then looked at the clock on the wall behind the counter. "Dang, we really do have to get out of here. We need to be back before Dad gets home!"

"Ohh," Lily moaned.

I paid the check, and we got ready to part ways. I did a little mind search before Hadley left. I wanted to know if she'd had a good time. Okay, I cheated. However, what I'd found on her mind wasn't of our time that we had just spent together. She was thinking of something as simple as her next meal, something I'd just taken for granted. Her thoughts were, *What do I make for Dad's supper? What is there at home to cook? I think we have four potatoes left and maybe a cube or two of chicken bouillon. I could make some kind of potato soup. That's going to have to do. Oh, I hope it's enough.*

I suddenly felt remorse, remorse over the fact that I had Mom's meatloaf waiting for me at home — and not just meatloaf but also salad, bread, potatoes and vegetables. Oh, and a drink. I usually just had water, but I could have milk, orange juice or tea. That was the thing. I had a choice. I doubted Hadley did.

I couldn't invite her and her sister to supper, but I knew they had to get back to their dad. I felt tremendously overwrought with guilt. *But what do I do for someone in Hadley's situation? How do I help her without making her feel embarrassed?*

This was something I would have to work out, a new challenge to add to the many I currently was facing. *Just what I need in my life right now...* Well, maybe it was.

Chapter Eight

Leftovers

At supper that night, I could hardly muster up an appetite. Mom knew right away something was up as she watched me play with my mashed potatoes, swirling them around on my plate.

"What's going on with you tonight?"

"Ohhh," I sighed. I caved. I told Mom everything about my new friend. I needed to tell somebody. Plus, I had a plan.

Mom and I discussed my idea. She thought it was a nice one. I figured she would. She's just too kind-hearted not to agree.

Mom dug out some old Tupperware. "I don't think I ever use this old stuff anymore. Why don't you put the leftovers in these?"

Dad, who had been sitting quietly through the whole conversation, grumbled a little as he watched Mom and me fill the containers, knowing that I was going to take away his favorite leftover food.

"Dad," I said as I gave him a side glance, "it's not like you need to eat any more." I mean, he was starting to get kind of a belly on him.

He grumbled and shook his head, but then looked back down at the newspaper he was reading.

I paused, walked over and gave him a little hug from the side. "Thanks, Dad."

He grumbled again, but smiled as he flipped out his paper, like he was still mad. *Yeah right. He really is a big softy too.*

Mom gave me a bag. I put all the leftover-filled Tupperware carefully on a shelf inside the refrigerator.

"Stay out, Dad," I said as I closed the refrigerator door.

He merely peered over the top of his newspaper.

"For real!" I reiterated.

Mom laughed. "It will be fine, Michael."

"Better still be there in the morning," I mumbled under my breath.

I checked the fridge one more time before bed. Dad had stayed clear of my leftovers. I was actually pleasantly surprised. I'd figured he would get into them when I was up in my room working on my homework. However, he'd behaved.

* * * *

Morning came none too soon. A night of tossing and turning had made for a twisted mess of bed covers. My thoughts had been filled with images of Hadley and Lily. I could see them standing in the dirt road in front of me, dressed in old clothes, tattered and drab. Both girls looked as if they belonged in a World War II concentration camp.

Emaciated images of Lily and Hadley had haunted me through the night. Even though I knew it wasn't that bad, I think my own guilt at having it so good was playing with my mind.

I had set my alarm for an hour earlier than normal. My plan was to leave the bag of food on Hadley's porch before she awoke.

I gathered Mom's leftovers. *I hope they don't just throw these away. I might if I didn't know where they came from. That is kind of weird. Um, well, maybe not if I was really hungry.* I went through the pantry. I added several cans of extra food. We had so much. I added two cans of chili, two cans of tuna, vegetable soup, a box of rice, two boxes of mac and cheese and some small packs of instant oatmeal.

I decided to jot a short note to leave with the leftovers, just in case.

Hadley, these are for you. Safe to eat and good too. Enjoy.

I didn't sign it, left it anonymous. Like she wouldn't know anyway.

All in all, it ended up being two bags of food, but grocery bags are pretty small these days. That was what I would tell Mom if she asked about the missing groceries.

The sun was just rising above the horizon as I headed out. Shades of orange rays shot across the blue sky. I loved this time of the morning. I found it to be particularly calming. No wind. No morning traffic yet. I jogged down the dirt road with my grocery bags in hand.

I wasn't even met by the barking dog. The beast must have been still asleep. I walked clandestinely down the row of shanties, like a cat on the prowl. I'm sure I looked ridiculous, especially since I was carrying two grocery bags.

A few lights were on already, but all in all, it was quiet. A wood-burning stove was lit in one shanty and it smelled like a campfire. That made the place seem idealistic somehow, though I knew it wasn't.

Hadley's little shanty already had a light on. I would have to be careful, remembering how creaky the little porch was.

Creeaaaak! The old, rickety wooden step broke the peaceful silence of the morning. I stopped in my tracks and looked around. My position seemed safe. I crept closer to the door and placed the bags down, hoping I had not given myself away.

A flash of light from the parting of the curtains caught my eye. Lily's little face was pressed against the glass. *Shit! Busted!*

"Shh-h," I raised my finger to my lips and shook my head.

Lily gave me an evil glare, then she looked down to the two bags at the door. She looked back at me. I stood, waiting for her verdict. Finally, she gave me a hint of a smile and nodded.

I took off at a fast pace. I knew Lily would immediately open the door to inspect the bags. I didn't want to have to explain them to Hadley, nor did I want Hadley to feel embarrassed. I was sure, however, that the subject would be questioned later.

I was trying to look back one more time before rounding the corner of the last shanty.

Blam!

Dang, not again.

I ran right smack into somebody. At least this time I didn't knock them to the ground.

The man was hefty in stature. Unkept. Unclean. He smelled of rotten cheese and vinegar. He was a loathsome being.

"What are you doing here?" the gruff voice asked.

Instantly I was sensing a malevolent aura. My instincts told me to get away.

Before I could react, the man grabbed me by my shirt collar in one hand and was wielding a knife in the other. "Have any money on ya?"

I did, but this thug wasn't getting it.

"No!"

"Yeah, right. Hand it over, kid. Everything!"

I grabbed the man's hand that was holding my shirt. I pushed it away with a mighty force. An astonished look came over his face. He was caught off guard. His only reaction was to send his knife-wielding hand forward. He drove it toward my chest, but he was too slow.

I was quick to grab his wrist with such brute strength that I felt his bones crack within my grip. My instincts had taken over now — no thinking, just my body reacting, as prey would when being hunted. *Survival!*

I attacked the man with beastly force and impaled my teeth into his pulsating carotid artery, causing both of us to tumble to the ground.

Rancid! I spewed the blood out onto the ground. This man's blood was so full of alcohol that it seemed there was no good blood to drink. It was disease-ridden. The man wasn't long for this life. *What a waste.*

I knelt over his body and looked down at his face. He was still alive, but not for long. He reached up to me, tried to speak, but couldn't. His eyes were now filled with remorse.

It was too late. Blood sprayed out from the torn artery in the man's neck. I couldn't drink it, so I had to kneel there at his side while he bled out on his own.

I held his shoulders down and kept staring into his dying eyes. *Please just die already.* I felt badly now for this downtrodden man, but what was I to do?

Finally, the life was gone from his body. It was strange as I looked into his eyes — life there one moment then gone, just like that, like the wind had just taken it away somewhere and left only an empty shell. The man did leave behind a reminder of a mess. However, as I looked down, I found a remarkable pattern of blood now covering my shirt. Once again I was adorned in blood.

My shirt was not redeemable. I looked down to my jeans, the ones I had just purchased from the thrift store. *Maybe savable.*

Crap! I checked my phone. Forty minutes until school started. Now I had a body to get rid of and I had to get cleaned up too. I wiped the splattered blood off my face and looked down at my blood-soaked hand. *What a mess — and man, does this man's blood reek.*

The good thing was that this side of town was close to the edge of the forest. I slung the now-limp body over my shoulder. My new-found strength did come in handy. I looked around, forgetting that somebody could have been watching, but luckily, everything seemed quiet. Only a lone sparrow chirped at me from a nearby tree. I gave it a glare. Amazingly it piped right down. Even in this mess, I chuckled.

No roads. Straight into the trees behind the shanties, only one main road to cross. I would have to wait for a clearing in traffic, but there should be no problem this early in the morning.

I went at full pace. The shrubs were beating across my arms and face like an old leather whip. I figured I was getting plenty of scratch marks. If, like the gun wound, it would heal, I'd have no worries. Still, though, it didn't feel so good at the time, but time was one thing that I didn't have.

I quickly came upon the main road that separated me from town and the forest, the forest that Mr. Branikov had taken me to, the one with the deep limestone crevasse.

I paused at the road, hidden in the foliage, waiting for a car-free moment. It was a clear view of the road to my right, but a hill to my left. At the moment, a truck was passing by. I waited for its taillights to disappear then looked left. *Clear.* Right? Nothing as far as the hilltop.

I took off across the road with the body in tow. Lights crested the hill right as I crossed the midline of the road. *Oh, that's perfect!* I shot across into the thickness of the forest, hiding behind a tree, stopping to see what the vehicle would do. *Did they see me?*

The vehicle slowed as they neared my earlier spot in the road. I concentrated hard on the driver's thoughts. *What was that? A bear? No, bigfoot*, the driver laughed. *Oh, maybe it was just a deer.* The car drove on.

Geezus! That was close. I rearranged the lifeless body on my shoulder. It seemed to be becoming a much heavier load, but I trudged onward into the forest. Running now. I could feel time ticking away. Turning here and there, I lost my way several times and had to backtrack. This wasn't helping my time situation. Finally, I reached the limestone outcropping.

I told the lifeless man that I was sorry. I'm not sure why. Then I threw his body down the deep, dark crevasse, listening for a sound. Nothing. I could only imagine how deep this hole in the earth could be. Maybe it led straight to the depths of Hell. I imagined a heap of bodies. The thoughts of Hell made me shiver. *Hmm, hope that's not where I'm headed. Oh man, I've got to do better somehow.* I was definitely a mess, but I was working on it. Things just kept getting screwed up.

I checked the time again. Fifteen minutes left. This was going to be impossible. I was going to be late for school. I still had to sneak home, get cleaned up and get rid of the blood-soaked shirt.

Chapter Nine

His or Hers Bathroom

Luckily Dad had left for work and Mom was well on her way to meet with her usual group of lady friends for coffee. I wasn't sure what to do with my bloody shirt, so I did the Spray 'n Wash thing and threw it in the laundry with some of my other dirty clothes.

I left the washer running as I took off for school. Mom always left my clothes alone. That was our deal. She'd gotten tired of washing my clothes and immediately finding them back on the floor, so we'd made a pact—or she had. I would wash my own clothes. No more issues that way. I noticed that I didn't throw quite as many clean clothes around anymore. I was more careful now that I had to do my own laundry. *No wonder Mom used to get so mad about the wash. Hmm, and I was too dimwitted to figure it out.* I was way more appreciative now.

I wondered how my shirt would come out. It was so blood-soaked. Scary. Hopefully, it wouldn't ruin the entire load of clothes. *Oh well, too late to matter now.* I had to get to school.

I missed my first class. Of course, Callie met up with me at my locker. "You missed the Trig quiz. Mr. Elder gave it to us right off. I think he did it because he saw you were missing. He's such a jerk sometimes."

As I was reaching for my American history book, I shook my head in disgust. "Figures!"

"Where were you anyway?"

"Um, long story. I'll fill you in later." *What am I really going to tell Callie?*

"All right, you can tell me all about it at lunch," Callie said, then she hustled off down the hall, giving me a wave.

"See ya in a minute," I hollered. Callie was in my history class, but obviously she wasn't going to be late on my behalf. "Ohh-h," I sighed quietly. I needed to relax for a minute. *Geez, what a morning already. Oh, Mr. Branikov, how do you cope?*

Second class done. Third class coming up. My head was spinning. The day was going fast. Hadley would be in this class. *Will it be awkward? What will she say about the leftovers? Dang, maybe I shouldn't have.*

I stepped through the classroom door. Hadley was already there, sitting in the back. She gave me a little wave and a smile. *Oh, thank goodness.* "Phew."

I tossed my book down on the desk and plopped down with utter exhaustion in the chair next to Hadley.

She looked over with a frown. "Geez, you look like you're having a bad day, bruh, and it's only third period." She laughed.

"Grrr!" I growled at her, but I gave her a smile. "Phew." I shook my head.

Drrriiinnngg! The bell rang, signaling that it was time for class to start.

"Later," I whispered, just as Mrs. V, which was short for a last name that is really long and hard to pronounce, got up from her desk.

"Lunch," I mouthed.

A wide smile came over Hadley's face. She nodded yes then slid something out of her backpack that was lying under her chair. It was one of mom's Tupperware containers. *Cool.* I grinned back and gave her a thumbs up. It was nice that she would actually have something to eat at lunch when she joined the rest of us.

Now I couldn't wait for lunch. How quickly I'd forgotten about the lifeless body that I had struggled with just that morning. It already seemed so long ago.

Drrriiinnngg!

Fourth class came and went. I don't even remember what Mr. Gaskill talked about. At least I wrote down the assignment, but that's about all I did. I mean, economics, right? Not very exciting, unless you are someone like Jonathan maybe. I would get him to help me. He always guided me in this particular subject. He loved doing it since it was so easy a class for him that he wasn't allowed to take it.

No pizza today for me. There was nothing better than fries and a salad. Cheap too. I quickly grabbed a table for five. It was easy. The lunchroom wasn't full. All the cool kids — the ones with more money — often ate elsewhere for lunch. However, those same kids always found their way back later in the hour, if only to harass the likes of us.

Jonathan, Junie and Callie were quick to join me. Hadley quietly sat down next to me. Lunch was going great. We brought Hadley into our conversations like she had been one of us all along. I could tell she was loving it. No one even mentioned that she had food today, although I knew everybody was wondering about it. I knew Callie recognized the Tupperware. I caught her giving me a look when Hadley put it on the table, but I gave her a look back. She knew not to say anything.

Dang it! I needed to go to the bathroom. That was a good way of ruining the moment for me. For the old Jenna to go to the bathroom, it was simple — for Michael, a bit more complicated.

The one good thing was that our school had a new wing. The new wing had a unisex bathroom. That was the one I always used. It was simpler and I wouldn't get harassed using that one. No questions.

The bad thing was that it was a way from the lunchroom and many of my classes. For me as Michael, it was tough to use the other restrooms. I wanted to use the boys', but a lot of the boys didn't accept me, plus it wasn't like I had the bottom half done yet. There was no standing to pee.

I couldn't go in the girls' bathroom. A lot of the girls didn't accept me either, since my top half was done and I was on the T. I seemed like a boy to many of them. They didn't want me in the girls' bathroom. Plus, since I had been on the T, my menstrual cycles had all but diminished, which I loved, but some of the girls at school were weirded out about the issue. I don't know how they even knew. It was difficult to keep anything secret in this dang school.

So that was that. I had one bathroom.

"Excuse me, guys... I'm going to have to go...you know." I looked at Callie with that look. She understood.

She laughed. "Oh, you better run."

"Yeah, thanks," I said.

Hadley, of course, was at a loss.

"Bathroom," Callie said to Hadley.

"Oh, but—" Hadley replied as she looked confused and pointed to the restrooms in the lunchroom.

I don't know what Callie said to her in explanation, as I had sprinted away by then, but I was confident that my friend wouldn't share my secret.

I returned in a timely manner. The north wing was abandoned during lunch hour, making it easy to get to the bathroom and back quickly. I'd basically run the whole way.

Jonathan had finished my fries while I was gone, and it had been only minutes.

"Hey! Bro!"

"Oh, sorry. I figured you were finished."

"Yeah right. I had just started, you French-fry thief. You owe me now… Like help with my economics assignment."

Jonathan perked up. "Well of course. Easy payback for a few fries. Plus, anything for a friend."

I laughed. He was so full of crap.

Hadley offered to share some of her wonderful leftover meatloaf.

I smiled. "You know, no thanks. I just had meatloaf last night."

Hadley chuckled. Callie, of course, gave me an eye roll.

Chapter Ten

Something Like Obi-Wan Kenobi

Mr. Branikov peeked his head into the door of my sixth period study hall. He waved for me to come with him and looked to Mrs. Botti to see if it would be okay. She nodded.

As soon as we were alone in the hallway, Mr. Branikov looked down at me with a serious glance. "Did you get rid of the body without too much trouble this morning?"

Dang, how does he know? I hadn't even been around him today. Were we really that connected?

"It was self-defense! And yes, I took it to the place you showed me, the place in the forest."

"I know it was self-defense, Michael. Don't get all mad. It's okay, but you do have to be more careful. You know, try to be more aware of your surroundings maybe."

I nodded. I knew I did, but things just kept happening. It wasn't like I planned for this stuff, but maybe that was his point. I needed to avoid getting into these situations in the first place.

"Um, what are we doing?"

Mr. Branikov smiled. "Taking care of your missed math quiz—and lesson number two."

We walked down the hall. I had no idea what Mr. Branikov was doing. I tried to read his thoughts, but he had me blocked somehow.

We stopped in front of the math classroom door. Mr. Branikov slowly opened it and peered into the room. The kids seemed to be silently working on a math problem. Mr. Branikov waved Mr. Elder over to the door. Mr. Elder stepped out into the hall with us.

"What can I help you with, Drakon?"

Mr. Branikov got right to the point. "You will let Michael make up the math quiz that he missed this morning."

"I would like to let Michael make up the trig quiz," Mr. Elder said as he looked down at me with a blank look on his face.

"He will sit in the back of your classroom and take it now. You will see no issues with this matter and you will not question why Michael missed your class today." Mr. Branikov stared harshly into Mr. Elder's eyes and used a firm and steady voice.

Sweet, Obi-Wan Kenobi mind control. Can I do this? I thought, forgetting that Mr. Branikov could still read my thoughts. He looked over at me. *"Yes, Michael, with practice. Actually, I imagine that you have already done this without even knowing it. However, to master the skill, it takes experience…and it is not to be misused."* He looked down at me with that insightful glance once again.

I nodded. I got it.

"Do you?"

"Come on in, Michael. Take a seat at the back. You can make up your test. Just leave it on the desk when you're done and return to your study hall." Mr. Elder was actually smiling at me. *Strange. He never does that. I definitely need to master this skill, but who do I practice on? Hmm-m?*

The trig quiz was obviously a review. Mr. Elder had certainly given the quiz because he had seen that I had been absent that morning. *Jerk!* Ha, the last laugh was on him. I aced it and he never had a clue what had come over him. *Gotta love my Mr. Branikov.*

But there was no more school drama that day, thank goodness. A kid can only handle so much. I hustled home. Mainly, I wanted to jog down the dirt road on the way to the gym, maybe happening upon Hadley.

I ran in the side door of the house that led straight into the kitchen, then tossed my backpack haphazardly onto the table, whistling a happy tune — an old Disney tune, that *Zip-a-Dee* song of some kind, I think. It made me feel good. Mom was baking something that smelled like banana bread. The aroma in the kitchen was comforting.

I grabbed an apple out of the fruit bowl to hold me over until the banana bread was ready. I plopped down in the chair at the kitchen table, releasing all my stresses from the day. "Hey, Mom."

Nothing. No reply. Mom walked over to the table as I remained slouched in my chair. She laid a neatly folded T-shirt on the table in front of me. I immediately sat up. *Oh shit! Mom finished my laundry!*

"I needed the washer, so I finished your load of clothes. Is there anything you want to tell me about this?"

I looked down at the folded shirt. I picked it up and held it out in front of me. I knew what it was, my blood-adorned shirt from that morning. *Nope, Spray'n Wash did not do the trick.* The shirt was still a blood-splattered mess. I don't know... It looked kind of cool, psychedelic-like.

I looked at the shirt, then up to Mom, only to find her looking at me with a disconcerted face. I looked back to the shirt. I sat there in an uncomfortable silence, as Mom stood there at the side of the table. *What should I say? Oh, I know, Obi-Wan Kenobi mind control. Would it work?* I hated to practice on my mother, but right now, I needed help.

I stared intensely at Mom. "Yes, Michael," she said as she gave me a puzzled look.

"You don't care about this shirt." I concentrated hard, trying to send Mom the thought as well.

I waited, watched for her reaction. Hopeful.

Then she pulled out the chair next to me and sat down. She chuckled a little, but she still had that look of concern. "I really don't care about your shirts, Michael, but I do care that it is covered with blood."

I groaned under my breath.

Mom started to raise her hand to my face. I knew she was just making sure I was okay, but still, come on. I'm like sixteen now. I quickly brushed her hand aside. "Mom!"

"But I just want to know you're okay. It's not the bullies again, is it?"

I rolled my eyes. "Mom...no!" Now the lies. "I did it at the gym. I was boxing, just a bloody nose. Geez. Don't get so freaky."

I waited. *Will she buy it? Obi-Wan didn't do me so good.* Mom looked at my face, shook her head and got up from the table. "Want some banana bread? I think it's ready."

Dang, she bought it – or did my mind control work? Who knows?

"Yeah, of course. Thanks, Ma."

Mom was still chuckling as she brought me a piece of warm banana bread with butter melting over the top, just the way I liked it.

"What?" I grumbled.

She looked at me, paused then replied, "Dang, sweetheart, that must have been a heck of a bloody nose. Next time duck, or keep your guard up, or whatever it is that you do when you box."

I looked at her with a most serious face, then finally I broke and busted up laughing. "Yeah, okay, Mom."

I kept the shirt. I would have to find something else to do with it. I couldn't keep throwing away bloody clothes. What if someone like a police detective ever tracked one back to me. *Hmm? Maybe tie-dye?* I wondered if something crazy like that would work. It wasn't like I could do any more damage to the clothes.

I stuffed down the banana bread, enjoying every bite, even though I knew by the look on Mom's face that she thought I was eating too fast. No matter. I finished up and quickly got on my way to the gym. I slowed my jog as I neared the shanties along the dirt road. There was no sign of Hadley. However, there were flashing lights. It looked like a local sheriff's vehicle and one of the town's police cars. Hopefully, I hadn't left any evidence. My pulse raced, and it wasn't from my run.

I slowed to see if I could see anything, but the shanties along the roadside were blocking my view. I definitely didn't want to snoop around, on the off-chance that the police might stop to question me. Nope, on I ran to the gym. I'd have to question Hadley tomorrow at school and get the low-down.

Chapter Eleven

Hadley's Demise

I looked for Hadley straight away the next morning. She was nowhere around. Now I began to worry. *Oh, man, I hope she's okay. I wonder what the police really wanted yesterday?*

I chatted with my friends, but my mind was obviously somewhere else. Lunchtime came and went and still no Hadley. I was in a gloomy mood.

"Earth to Michael," Callie said as she dropped her tray on the table right in front of me to get my attention.

"Oh...hey." I looked up at Callie and gave her a fake smile.

"Geez, really, dude?"

Jonathan and Junie sat down about that time.

"What's wrong with Michael?" Junie asked, right off the bat.

Geez, am I really that transparent?

"Oh, Michael misses Hadley. I think our boy is finally in love."

"What?" I angrily responded as I perked right up.

Junie laughed. "Oh yeah, no doubt."

Dang, were my friends on to something? Why was I feeling so blue? I did miss the girl for some reason. I didn't even really know her yet, but deep inside I wanted to get to know her more. I wanted to see her face—most likely dirty—her straggly hair and her ragged clothes. Somehow I liked her and all her mess, and I wanted her to like me back.

My friends had a good chuckle, but then they changed the subject, leaving me alone. I think they actually felt pity for me.

"She's probably just home sick for the day," Callie reassured me after a bit, obviously seeing that I was still worried.

I nodded yes, but I was really not relieved. I had already decided that after school I would go by Hadley's shanty and check on her and Lily. For now, though, I turned my thoughts back to my friends, hoping they would get my mind off things—and they did.

We enjoyed the lunch hour...until the notorious James and the boys showed up. We were minding our own business when a football came rolling over by my feet. *Really, again?* I bent over to pick it up, and yes, I was going to deflate it with my powerful grip. However, Noah, one of the boys, was quick to pick it up off the floor.

"Oh no you don't," he mumbled.

James walked up beside me, reached down and rudely grabbed a handful of my fries, that mind you, I was still working on. He tossed them at Jonathan. James then looked to Junie. "You still hanging out with this dweeb?"

Junie rolled her eyes and leaned back in her chair. Jonathan merely smiled, picked one of the tossed fries up from the table and ate it, over-emphasizing the goodness of the little French fry. We couldn't help but laugh. James, of course, found this all highly irritating.

I could sense James was going to do something far more terrible, so I acted quickly, trying to turn his anger toward me. "You're such an asshole, James."

He looked at me, but then something amazing happened. Instead of attacking me, he stood there silently for a moment like a dork then he said, "I am such an asshole."

What? Obi-Wan Kenobi, I love you, man. It had worked! It'd really worked — by accident, maybe, but my mind-control power had worked.

Everybody at the table and the boys standing around were shocked. I don't know how many mouths dropped open — too many to count.

I had some bottled tea sitting in front of me. I really didn't want to waste it, but I couldn't resist.

"I think you want to pour my tea over your head."

Callie, Jonathan and Junie were giving me a befuddled look. I just shrugged.

"I am going to pour this over my head and you can't stop me!" James said as he snatched up my bottle of tea.

"Um…okay." I chuckled under my breath.

To everybody's astonishment, James poured the tea over his always well-kept head of hair. He poured out the entire bottle. Raspberry tea was rolling down his face as he stood there in front of us, acting like he had done something fierce.

My friends and I were trying to keep it together, but we just couldn't. We busted up laughing, as did everyone else except for James' squad. They were clueless as to why James was acting this way. None of them knew what to do.

"Now, leave us alone!" I gave James a good-bye wave over my shoulder.

James gave us all a weird look. "We're leaving now," he simply said and turned to his squad. "Come on, guys."

Just like that, the group of miscreants were walking out of the lunchroom. I turned to watch them, but at the main door I caught a glimpse of something else. There stood Mr. Branikov. He had been watching — or was he helping? Dang, now I wasn't sure of myself.

"What was that all about?" Callie asked, still with a shocked look on her face.

I turned to reply to her then I glanced back at the main doors. Mr. Branikov was gone. However, James and the boys were on their way out. They seemed to be arguing. Now *that* was funny.

I turned back to my friends. They had a million questions.

"I don't know. I think James was on drugs or something. I just took advantage of the situation."

My friends all agreed it must have been the case. Come to find out, Junie had dated James. *No wonder we're suddenly having all the problems.* She told us that he had a lot of problems going on at home that nobody knew about. She didn't doubt that he might be drunk or high on something.

Well, another lunch hour over, another victory for us. I'd done my job well. I'd protected Jonathan once again and maybe this would help keep the thugs at bay — or maybe not — but I would be there if they came back around.

The afternoon classes passed slowly. School couldn't go by quick enough.

Drrriiinnngg! Finally, the last bell sounded. There would be no after-school chatter with my friends. I had things to do. I completed my usual routine at home, with one exception. I grabbed a grocery bag and threw in some fruit and some canned chicken noodle soup in case Hadley was really sick. Oh, and I tossed in a baggie full of Oreos, just because who doesn't like those? I was then out of the door, anxious to go find Hadley.

I slowed to a walk upon reaching shanty town. As I walked up the shanty row, I saw the remnants of some yellow crime-scene tape. *My last crime spot, indeed.* The tape, though, was already torn, blowing in the wind, disregarded. The scene had obviously been left abandoned by the police. It only figured that they would not give matter to any crime done in this area. They really didn't care about the likes of those who lived here, even if some were innocent, just down on their luck.

An old lady was sitting in front of her little shanty on an old wooden rocking chair. She smiled at me. I don't think she had many teeth left, poor thing. I gave her a little wave. She reminded me of my great-grandma, other than the teeth. Although, I think my great-grandma had dentures, so her teeth were maybe just as bad, only she could afford the fake ones.

I approached Hadley's shanty. The curtains were drawn, but I could see a light glimmering through the outer edges.

Creeaaaak! The rickety wooden step gave away my stealthy approach. Before I could knock, the door opened. There stood Lily.

"Michael! Did you come by to take us to get ice cream?"

I laughed. "No, not today, but…" I reached into the bag that I had brought along and pulled out the baggie full of Oreos. Lily wasted no time. She quickly snatched them out of my hand, smiled then ran away, leaving me standing awkwardly at the doorway.

"Hello?"

Finally, Hadley stepped forward into the light. "What are you doing here?'

"Geez, really? I don't know. I saw all the police lights yesterday, then you weren't at school. Um, so, just checking. You know, making sure you're okay, like friends do."

Hadley hemmed and hawed as she stared at the floor. "Oh."

I just stood there.

"Oh. Come in." Hadley pointed to the couch. "Um, you want something to drink?"

I smiled. "No, I'm good. Thanks, though."

Hadley giggled a little. "Good, because we only have water." She looked down at the bag I was carrying. "You shouldn't have brought anything."

"I thought you might have been sick."

About that time Lily showed up holding the baggie of Oreos and with one hanging half out of her mouth.

"Hey, I want one of those," Hadley said as she reached for her sister's hand. Lily, of course, was having none of that. She quickly jerked the baggie away.

I watched for the next several minutes as Hadley and Lily playfully fought for dominion over the Oreos. Hadley won, but in the end she took only one cookie, laughed at Lily then handed her the entire baggie back. With that, Lily was out of the front door. Gone, like a thief in the night, cookies in hand.

Hadley turned to me and, with a most serious face, she held out the Oreo and asked, "And you thought this would help me if I was sick?"

I laughed, then I pulled out the chicken noodle soup. "No! This."

"Ohh." Hadley laughed.

Hadley went on to tell me all about what had happened. She explained that someone had found a huge mess of blood at the corner of shanty row. She explained that the police had hardly given it a look-over and that it had infuriated her.

All while Hadley was talking, I was thinking, *Thank goodness. Like, good for my situation, but it was wrong of the police. If it had been the Woodland Heights, the ritzy part of town, the police would have been all over it.*

Hadley went on to explain, in an uneasy manner, that her dad had spent a lot of time at the bars lately, especially when he couldn't get any work at the day-labor line.

"But he always comes home by morning and he hasn't come home. It's been two days now, and with the blood, I'm really worried that something has happened. That's why I stayed home from school. I've been waiting for Dad. Like, what if he's hurt?"

My mind started racing. *A drunk. Shanty town. Comes back in the morning... Who did I kill?*

"Um, I'm sure he's okay. Maybe he found work and just stayed out." I tried to give Hadley something positive, but that was not what I was really thinking.

"No, Michael. Rent is coming up. Dad always gets enough money gathered up just in time to pay the rent. Something is wrong!"

"Hmm." I shrugged. I felt nauseated. "Did you tell the police?"

"I can't! If Dad is missing, they'll take Lily away. I can't tell anyone."

"Crap. That sucks." I didn't know what else to say. "What about the rent?"

Maybe that wasn't the best question to ask at the moment. Hadley was more worried about her dad. However, she did need to figure out a way to pay the rent, and I needed to figure out who it was that I'd killed.

Chapter Twelve

The Deepest, Darkest Hole

It was dark and dreary. I could see by the trash that lay at my feet that I was in the skanky part of downtown. The rain was pouring down. I couldn't keep the water from my eyes.

I rounded the corner of an old, run-down building. Kathud! Once again, I ran right into someone. I looked up, the rain still muddling my view. It was a man, hefty in stature, straggly, unkempt. Wait! This can't be. I killed you already!

I attempted to shove the man away, but he was having none of that. I struggled to see his face clearly. The rain was getting heavier with every moment. I caught a glimpse of a knife in the man's hand just as he lunged forward. Everything was repeating itself.

I stopped him with brutal force, just as before. It was an unfair battle. We fell to the ground as I ripped open his carotid artery. The blood bath began.

Wretched blood. *I knew this taste. Undrinkable. I knelt over the man as he looked up to me. Yes, it was the same guy! This time, I could hear his words as he reached out to me.* "Hadley, Lily."

"Shit!"

I sprang straight up in my bed, soaked in sweat. It was dripping into my eyes, like the rainwater from my dreams.

I knew. I knew that I had killed Hadley's dad—but still, I wanted proof, and my proof was at the bottom of some deep, dark crevasse.

Now guilt-ridden and full of sorrow for Hadley, I needed to find a way to help her. First, I had to make sure Hadley got her rent paid. There wasn't going to be any dad around to pay it, but I wasn't going to tell her that, not yet. *Dang, how will I ever let her know?* Second, I needed my friends to help me descend into the crevasse. I wanted to see if I could get to the bottom of things, so to speak.

Okay, first, the rent money. I had an idea. I had an old saxophone. I'd picked it up at a garage sale a while back from an elderly jazz player, Clyde Samuel. He'd told me he used to play at some old bar back in the fifties and sixties. I'd been like, "Dude, I wasn't even alive yet."

The man had given me a really good deal on the sax, but he'd made me promise him that I would learn to play it. I'd tried. I could never get the right jazz sound. I pretty much sucked. I figured that I had kept my promise. I had given the old sax a try, but now I needed it for something more important—for money, for Hadley.

It was a Conn New Wonder tenor saxophone. The old guy had told me it was a 'Chu Berry'. I didn't have a clue what that was, but I knew the sax was in great condition, had the original parts and the original case. I figured it would bring a pretty good sum.

The good thing was that it was Saturday morning, so there was no school. I waited for Mom and Dad to clear out of the house. I think they were headed out grocery shopping. I didn't want to have to explain anything.

I grabbed the old sax and headed out to the local pawn shop. It didn't take long, as getting anywhere in town was fast.

The big sign on top of the store read *Pawn & Guns*. Nothing like being original, but I guess they didn't have to. I think it was the only pawn shop in town.

The little bell on the door jingled as I walked in toting my sax. I walked up to the counter and gently placed the saxophone case on the counter. A middle-aged man peered over. "What are you up to, kid?"

Duh? What does he think?

"Well, I have this old thing and I've decided to get rid of it."

"How old are you?" the man asked with one eyebrow raised at me.

"What?" I asked, then I arrogantly added, "Sixteen." *Like, duh.* This man was making me mad.

"Your parents know you're here?"

"Of course," I lied.

"Hmm...okay."

I could sense that the man knew what the case was and he was interested in what might be inside.

"Let's see what you have there." The man started to open the case.

I slid it away from him, if only to torment him a bit. "This is a cash deal and I know what it's worth, so don't try to swindle me," I lied again.

The man looked at me with a squinted gaze, then he chuckled. "Okay, okay, kid, but let's see the thing."

I opened up the case and slid it forward for him to examine. I concentrated on his thoughts. He wanted the sax. There was no doubt. Twenty-eight hundred dollars entered his thoughts. *Whoa! That's awesome.* I tried to hold my excitement as I now knew what the sax was worth.

"Yeah, it's okay, but it's really not what I'm looking for," the man said, trying to hide his own excitement.

"Oh, all right," I shrugged and started to close the case like I was going to take it away.

The man put his hand on the case. "Oh, but wait. I can probably take it off your hands for a little bit of cash."

I looked at the man. Stood there. Didn't say anything. Waited for his price.

"Well, I suppose that I could give you four hundred bucks. That's a lot of money, you know, for a kid," the man tried to coax me.

What a crook!

I laughed in an obnoxious manner. "Yeah, I don't think so. I told you, mister. I know what it's worth. Um, what do you think, twenty-eight hundred or so?"

The man looked astonished, like I had read his very thoughts — which I had.

"Geez, kid." I started to close the case again. "All right, all right, but I have to make *some* money here, ya know."

I smiled. I was actually so excited that I was having a hard time holding back. I had only paid old Clyde twenty-five bucks for the thing. "All right, two thousand dollars. I know you can still make money. The thing is in like mint condition and has all the original stuff. So, two thousand, take it or leave it. Oh, and that little charm bracelet there too," I said as I pointed to a small bracelet that was under the glass counter. I then added my mind control, just in case it might work. It was worth a try.

The man stared at me, then at the sax, then back to me.

"Damn, kid, you're killing me. All right, two thousand…and the stupid bracelet."

Mind control? Or just good bargaining?

The man counted out the hundred-dollar bills. One hundred, two hundred, three — and finally two thousand. Then he brought out the bracelet from the counter and practically slammed it down onto the glass top. I quickly snatched it up and put it into my pocket before he changed his mind.

I looked down at the stack of money. *Dang, I've never had so much money in my life. This is so sick!*

I could surely help Hadley with her rent now. The question would be how to do so without hurting her feelings. I would have to figure that out later.

Now I had to get on with part two, getting to the bottom of things. I knew the gym had some rock-climbing gear. I would just have to borrow it for a day or two. No one ever used it. I doubted they would ever know it was missing.

The hard part was that I would need, at minimum, the help of Callie and Jonathan. I needed them to help with the ropes as I descended into the crevasse, especially if something were to go wrong. I didn't want to be lost in some deep, dark hole with no one ever knowing about it.

What would I tell my friends was the reason behind this madness? *I know, a school research paper. Yeah, something special for my Earth and Science class. Something to do with the study of limestone caverns.* I wasn't sure. It was pretty weak, but I figured I would just make it up as I went along.

I stopped by the gym. Rather than steal — or I mean 'borrow' the rock-climbing stuff — I figured I would first ask old man Lockey. He ran the place. He found my whole school paper story fascinating. I didn't exactly tell him that I was planning on descending into a deep, dark crevasse that might be endless. I might have used a little mind control, not sure, but whatever… Mr. Lockey gladly gave me use of all the equipment.

"Just bring it back when you're done with it, Michael. Oh, and don't break a leg or anything. I don't want any trouble over this."

I assured him that it was between me and him, and that there would be no trouble. He seemed not to even give it another thought. I knew it would have been a huge liability for the gym, so he must have been listening to my thoughts. *This is so cool*, I thought as I gathered up the equipment. *I am like so savage*. It would be interesting to see how long my brashness would last.

I found Callie, Jonathan and Junie all at the library on Sunday. *What a bunch of nerds*. No wonder they were smarter than the rest of us.

"Hey, what's up?" I interrupted their intense study group.

"Shh!" Callie put her finger up to her lips and gave me an eye roll. "This is the library, dude," she whispered.

I knew that, but they were the only ones in the place. I tilted my head at her. I sighed.

Callie nodded then pulled out the chair next to her and across the table from Jonathan and Junie, inviting me to sit down. Jonathan and Junie peered up from their studies. I could see that the two were playing footsie under the table. *They're so funny*.

Callie whispered, "What do you need? It must be important, guys, for Michael to come around the library."

"Whatever," I mumbled as I sat down at the table.

I laid out my plan for my friends. After I was done, they mostly laughed, thinking I was crazy — and maybe I was. At first Jonathan thought that I was joking. I had to reassure all of them that I was really going to do this.

"But, guys, it has to be a secret. I want my school project to be one of a kind. No one can know." This was one whopper of a lie.

"Since when have you cared so much about Mrs. Heckendorn's class?" Callie was definitely questioning my intentions.

I explained to my friends that this was just something I had been wanting to do, and the school paper had given me an excuse to do so. They somehow bought off on that being more likely.

The good thing was that I could sense the three of them were also intrigued by my search of this so-called 'crevasse to hell'. It was something they hadn't even known about. They were always up for an adventure, so in the end, they were in.

"Let's go now!" Jonathan said as he slammed his chemistry book closed.

Junie slapped him on the shoulder. "We can't go now. You haven't finished your AP chemistry worksheet yet, dork."

Jonathan slumped back in his chair and looked up to me with a face that said, 'I'm sorry, bro'.

"Hmm? How about tomorrow after school? We have enough daylight hours to get this done, I think." I looked around at my friends and waited for their answer.

My friends hemmed and hawed, discussed it for a few moments then finally agreed they would do it, which I'd known all along they would. They just wanted to torture me and take their time about it. Little did they know that I could sense their thoughts now. I chuckled.

"How about Hadley?" Callie asked, "You going to invite her along?"

"No!"

Callie looked at me, wide-eyed.

"A secret, guys. This has to remain a secret."

"Ooh, mysterious." Callie mocked me, but she grinned. "Okay, a secret, Michael. We got it."

Chapter Thirteen

The Hole to Hell

We met at the baseball field bleachers. My backpack was void of schoolbooks. No room. The rock-climbing gear took up almost the entire backpack. Plus, I'd thrown in a half-empty pack of cookies that I'd grabbed out of the pantry that morning. I didn't want to have to listen to how hungry Jonathan was the entire time.

I'd stuffed four water bottles into the outside pouches of the backpack. I doubted my friends would think to bring anything. The side pocket held a flashlight. I'd put in new batteries the night before, just to be safe. I was ready for this descent into darkness.

We walked down a side road to the edge of town. The forest started just across the highway.

"You sure about this?" Callie asked as we all stood by the road looking at the thick, dark forest on the other side.

"Oh yeah. I've been here a lot. No problem."

My friends all looked at me. I could sense an abundance of doubt flowing through their thoughts.

When traffic cleared, we made a break for it. Junie spoke out as we made it to the other side. "You've been here a lot?" Jonathan and Callie looked at me with curiosity as well.

"Um, well, maybe not a lot. Some, though."

They all stood there, not sure about this. Callie had her hands on her hips, like she was a little mad at me. I went on to explain. "You know, just exploring and stuff."

"Hmm," Callie mumbled.

However, even with their doubt, my friends followed me. We trampled through the thick foliage. The undergrowth was annoying and wet. I hadn't realized on my previous journeys just how treacherous this forest really was. The past two trips, the first with Mr. Branikov and the second with the last body, were more of a blur, all done with adrenaline. I hadn't paid attention to the details.

"Holy crap, Michael! Where in Hell are you taking us?" Callie complained.

Indeed, am I taking us to Hell?

We wandered a bit. I was just stalling as I seemed to be a little lost. We stopped for a break. Luckily I had the cookies and the water. They were much-needed and appreciated. Plus, it kept my friends from lynching me at the moment.

"Okay, Michael, enough already. How much farther?" Callie asked.

"Yeah, bruh, you're almost out of cookies already," Jonathan added as he stuffed another one into his mouth.

"What?" I grabbed the bag from him. Dang if he hadn't eaten almost all of them. "Geez, bro, really?" I rolled my eyes.

"Well, whatever, but like Callie asked, how much longer? Where is this place? Do you even know where we are? Man, we're all going to die out here."

I lied, kind of. I knew we were close. I just had to find the place exactly. The thick foliage kept everything well hidden. "We're close. Geez, Jonathan, don't get your panties in a wad."

Jonathan picked up a rock and threw it at me. It was quite the pathetic throw, but that didn't matter — with my cat-like reflexes, I easily caught it. I looked down at the rock in my hand. Limestone. We were close! *Hmm, which way, though?*

I concentrated on the rock formation. I knew I could sense it, feel it. I had to trust my gut, my instincts.

"This way."

I led my friends forward — or maybe to the side. It all looked the same in the forest. Dang, if the rock outcropping wasn't but a hundred yards from where we'd taken a break.

"Really, Michael? Why didn't we just wait and take a break here?" Callie asked as she gave a big huff and sat down on one of the rocks. She gave me a side glance with piercing eyes. I think she guessed that I had been lost earlier.

I ignored her question. "Careful, guys! There's a big-ass hole right there." I pointed to the crevasse, which was actually very well hidden amid the limestone outcropping.

Of course everybody had to go and peer in. Jonathan threw a rock down into the darkness. We listened. I could hear it at first as it banged against the walls of the crevasse, but then…nothing. Silence!

"Dang, bro. I don't know. Are you sure you want to go down there? What if there's no bottom?"

I looked at Jonathan. "Well, that's what I am going to find out. And that's why you guys are here, to make sure I get back out."

I dumped the rock-climbing gear out onto a flat surface of limestone, where we could see it clearly and where it was off the mucky forest floor. Jonathan and Junie were quick to set up a rappelling system. That was what I had hoped for. I'd known that if I invited these two, they wouldn't be able to resist. They would have had to research the task that I was doing, so that they would be the ones to know all about it. Yes, I was using my friends. It's nice to have genius friends sometimes.

I put on the climbing harness and some of Dad's old leather gloves. I barely knew what I was doing. *Oh man, I'm going to kill myself.* I found it amusing that only the previous year I had tried to fall from the town bridge, trying to kill myself for real, and now that I might fall, I didn't particularly want to. I now wanted to live. *Funny how quickly things turn around in life if you just give them a chance.*

Junie and Jonathan had a brake system on the rope and it was anchored around one of the nearby trees. They were planning to use a belay device. My descent would be entirely in their hands. *Oh crap, nothing scarier than that.*

I didn't know enough about ascending to get back out, so I would have to rely on my friends. The gear was there, a Petzl rope clamp and some Grivel ascenders, but I didn't have a clue how to use them. Death was knocking at my door. Hopefully with the tree as an anchor and my three friends pulling the rope, they would manage to get me back out. *This will be an interesting adventure.*

I stuck the flashlight in my front jeans pocket as best I could. It wasn't great, but hopefully it would stay. This could definitely turn into a debacle if I wasn't careful.

Down I went into the darkness — ten yards, twenty, fifty. The light above was becoming a narrow slit. It became darker and colder as I descended. It was creepy for sure.

Callie stayed at the edge of the crevasse and talked to me as I descended, making sure everything was going okay. It was calming to hear her voice. If not for that, I feared there would be nothing down there. *Maybe this is a hole to Hell.*

Farther and farther down I went, touching the walls of the crevasse just to feel like something was still there. I was beginning to wonder if there would be enough rope. Callie hollered something, but her voice was becoming distorted, faint. I'm sure my voice was no better as I hollered back up from time to time, letting them know I was okay.

There was total darkness now. I couldn't see anything, not even my hand in front of my face. I could feel the dampness in the air and it had gotten much cooler. Then I got a whiff of a smell, a foul odor, unlike anything that I knew. It smelled something like rotting meat mixed with rotten eggs and spoiled fruit. *Eww.* It smelled worse than one of those rotting animals on the side of the road and the odor was getting heavier in the air as I descended.

My feet touched something. First, I jumped. It scared the bejesus out of me. *Crap! Is it the bottom?* I finally gathered my senses. Whatever it was, it was soft. I moved my feet back and forth, pushing slightly down. It was solid. As the tension on the rope loosened, I put my weight down on one foot, then the other. Yes, firm ground.

"Off belay!" I screamed up to the crevasse opening as loud as I could, hoping Callie could hear me.

I reached for my flashlight in a panic, with no idea as to what the soft, mushy ground was that I was standing upon. Thank goodness, it was a relief that I found the flashlight still safely tucked away in my pocket.

Click! The light shone into the darkness. My eyes took a moment to adjust. The crevasse appeared to be a long, narrow cavern, with nothing but walls of limestone. I moved the light slowly down to my feet, not really wanting to see what was there.

I puked. Cookie remnants splattered at my feet. At least it took away from the horrid odors rising from the cavern floor. I wiped my mouth with my sleeve. After a moment, I mustered up enough bravery to look back at what my light had revealed.

It was the man I had thrown into the crevasse only a few days before. This body, though, was already atrociously decayed, beyond what I'd expected of a normal one. *Not that I'm an expert, but holy crap, really?* If it weren't for the same clothes of the man that I had struggled with and killed, I might not have recognized the face. I shone the light closer, just to make sure it was him.

Something small and black crawled out of the man's mouth, a beetle of some sort. I was caught off guard and, yes, I puked again—more like gagged, as there was nothing left to throw up. "Geez! Really? Anything else?" I said out loud in anger.

Once I settled down a bit, I noticed several more beetles scurrying away from the light. Now I understood why the body had decayed so quickly. It was the damn bugs! *Hmm, maybe Drakon knows this. Maybe that's why he uses this place. Quick removal of evidence.* I'd also recalled a science lesson, which was funny to me, that school had actually come in handy. *Lime, which is plentiful in these limestone caverns and enhances the speed of decay. That is, it leads to the rapid and total destruction of human bodies. Oh, Drakon, you are a genius.*

I shone my light around the narrow cavern. There were no other obvious creatures to be seen. However, I sensed several things lurking in the darkness, but nothing to be afraid of. I sensed more fear coming from them, whatever they were.

I walked only a little way from the body, crunching a few old bones under my feet. That was enough for me. Back to the man's body. I needed his wallet.

I turned the body on its side. It practically fell apart. More beetles scurried away, causing me to dance around a little. *Good thing my friends weren't here to see that.* I managed to get back to my task at hand. It was by far the grossest thing I had ever done.

I dug into the man's back pocket and pulled out his wallet. I flipped through it. No money. *Figures.* A picture of two little girls with the man. "Geez, dude, you're killing me." Now I was talking to the dead guy. *Great.*

As I studied the picture, I recognized that it was him with Hadley and Lily from long ago. I quickly stuffed the picture into my pocket, as it was torture to look at. Finally, a driver's license, which was expired. That didn't surprise me. "Mr. Johnson, you weren't doing so well in life, were you?"

I knew for sure now. It was what I had feared all along. Indeed, it was Hadley's dad. I didn't want to keep the wallet. It stank of death. I took everything that was inside it, which wasn't much, and stuffed that into my pocket, along with the photo of the girls that was already there.

That was enough for me. *Get me out of this wretched place!*

Oh yeah, class project. Let's see. I snapped a few photos of the cavern, making sure to leave out all traces of any bones or bodies. Then I tried to take a photo of some beetles, but they kept scurrying away. I finally smashed one with an old bone that I picked up—a leg bone, I think. No matter, it did the trick. I made sure not to totally obliterate the bug. I wanted a good enough photo that maybe I could identify it, like for a real class project. That might come in handy someday.

"On belay!" I screamed at the top of my voice. Nothing. I didn't think my friends could hear me. I tried waving the rope, but it was too long, so the wave wasn't making it to the top. I thought I could see a profile of a head in the narrow slit of light above me. That had to be Callie. I waved my flashlight back and forth. Nothing.

Come on, guys. Get me out of this grave!

I was losing my patience. *How long did they think I wanted to be down here? Come on. You're supposed to be the smart ones.*

I shone my light around the cavern. The beetles! Where were they all scurrying to? It seemed like they were all going in the same direction.

I unhooked myself from the carabiner and started following the bugs. It was narrow, dark, smelly and wet. *Nothing appealing about any of this.* I probably should have just waited for my friends, but I'd gotten too impatient. *Stupid.*

I slid through a point where I had to suck in my gut all the way, barely sliding through and scraping some of my skin from my hip bones. Not pleasant.

The narrow passageway gave way, opening into a larger cavern. There was no overhead opening. Something stirred. *Shit! Bats!*

They were not happy to be awoken. They started stirring and screeching. I immediately crouched down into a ball. I didn't want any bat biting me. Why was I worried? What? *Are they going to turn me into a vampire or something? Ha!*

I turned off my light to try to calm them down, but it was too late. However, I was amazed at how well I could see in the dark cavern. Once my eyes adapted to the darkness, I wasn't sure I even needed a flashlight. I could see more details in the cavern than I could see before—every line in the rocks, every bug that was crawling along the ground and a few remaining bats that were still circling above.

The rest of the bats had flown out of the narrow slit from which I'd come. I assumed they were headed out the cavern opening. *Oh crap! I hope Callie doesn't have her head hanging over the hole.*

With the bats gone, the place became quiet once again. Loneliness set in as I realized the cavern was a dead end and it was just me and the creepy beetles. I headed back to the rope.

Luckily it was still there. I had worried that my friends might have tried to pull it up when I was gone, but they had not. I hooked back into the carabiner then screamed to no end. I tried my phone, no signal.

Finally, I broke off some pieces of limestone rock. Thank goodness for my strength. I hadn't tried throwing anything, but what the heck. I had nothing to lose. I catapulted the rock with all my might. It shot up through the darkness with bullet speed. I imagine it went way too far. *Oh shit! I hope I didn't hit anybody. Didn't think about that.*

Okay, maybe the rock thing wasn't such a good idea. I stood there in the darkness thinking about it for a while. *Duh, Obi-Wan Kenobi mind stuff.* I concentrated hard, trying to send my thoughts to Callie. *I'm done. I'm done. Get me out of here!*

The rope moved. Finally, my friends—or at least Callie—had gotten the message. I was on my way out. Slowly I ascended the limestone walls. As I reached the top, Callie was there waiting for me. She immediately started beating on me. I wasn't sure why. Okay, bats, maybe.

"Hey! Help me out first at least," I said as I was still hanging halfway in the hole.

Callie stopped and finally gave me a hand, pulling on my shoulders. With that, I managed to hoist myself the rest of the way out. I slowly rolled over, got up and dusted off my now-filthy pants. I took a deep breath and stood to face my three friends, who were now lined up like a firing squad. I sensed that they weren't happy.

However, the mood changed quickly as they took one look at me. The expressions on their faces morphed. Callie's mouth dropped open.

"What?" I asked as they all stared at me.

After an uncomfortable moment of silence, Jonathan finally said, "Bro, your eyes!"

I quickly bent back over. I knew my eyes hadn't yet adjusted to the light, because things were still a little blurry. I stared at my shoes. I concentrated until every detail came back into focus.

I stood back up. "What?" I asked again.

My three friends were still staring at me.

"No way," Junie mumbled.

Callie walked up to me and grabbed my chin, turning my face toward her. "Strange." Her eyes were piercing into mine.

"Guys...what?"

"Bro, you had... I don't know." Jonathan shrugged.

Junie butted in. "You had cat eyes, like for real. I swear you did...but they're gone now."

"Hmm." I shrugged. "Must have been the darkness." I tried to brush it off. Then I tried to change the subject. "Um, did you see the bats?"

Callie gave me a big shove. Undoubtedly, she'd had a run in with the bats.

"You jerk. Was that your doing?"

I looked at her with an innocent face and shrugged.

"Creep," she mumbled.

"Now wait. You're not getting off the hook that easy. I know what I saw! Your eyes were not normal," Junie said as she crossed her arms in a huff.

I really didn't know what my eyes had looked like. I did remember Drakon telling me during one of my lessons that I would have cat-like vision and that it would help me see better at night. *What did Drakon say exactly? 'Panther-like vision.' Is that what my eyes looked like to my friends? Did I have the eyes of a panther? Hmm...cool.*

"Yeah, Michael, what's been going on with you lately? Are you taking too much testosterone?" Callie asked.

I looked at her and scowled. "Of course not!"

"Then what is happening?"
Do I tell them? They are my best friends, after all.

Chapter Fourteen

Nosferatu

I dumped out the contents of my pocket. Jonathan, Junie and Callie looked at the few items in the pile. They all shrugged, as if to say 'what are we looking at?'. They were not impressed. I picked up the old photo of Hadley, Lily and her dad and stuck it in front of my friends' faces.

Callie looked closely at the photo. She got it. "Hey, that's Hadley!"

I nodded.

"What does that mean? You got this from down in that hole?"

I nodded again. I picked out Mr. Johnson's license from the pile and held it out for my friends to see.

"Hadley's dad?" Junie asked.

"Yes."

My friends all stood there, silently looking at me, taking it all in, waiting for me to say something.

What the hell am I doing? How do I tell my friends this next part?

"Hadley's dad's body is down there. I got you guys to help me because I needed proof that it was him."

I held out the license once again.

"What? Huh?" my friends all mumbled and scowled.

Callie was rather perturbed. "You used us!"

I shrugged then smiled a little. "Well, it's not like you guys didn't want a little adventure. Like, what else were you going to do today?"

I think Callie was going to attack me, but Junie stopped her. "No, Callie, Michael's right. We wanted to come. It was more fun than sitting around the library all afternoon. But, Michael, tell us this. How did you know Hadley's dad was down there?"

Okay, here comes the hard part.

"Well, I threw his body down there."

My friends were all shocked and eerily quiet. I don't think they knew what to say, and that wasn't like them at all. I guessed I understood why, though.

I went on to explain. I started with the day that I'd run into Mr. Johnson. I explained that it was self-defense. I told them that the man had pulled a knife on me and was going to rob me. I gave them all the details—well, almost. I left out the main fact for later. I wasn't sure just how much my friends could handle.

"But this is so confusing, Michael. How did you overcome a grown man and how could you have gotten his body here? This doesn't make any sense." Callie focused her eyes upon me.

"Um, do you guys know what a Nosferatu is?"

Callie looked at me as if she were clueless. However, Jonathan and Junie busted up laughing. They knew.

"What are you trying to say?" Junie asked as she was still laughing.

I asked my friends if they remembered a few years back when I was having a lot of problems with my identity issues. They nodded. I went on to tell them the entire story, from the leaping off the town bridge to awakening with a new-found life. I told them everything.

At first they were giggling, thinking I was joking, but as I continued, they began to listen more intently. I sensed they were actually starting to believe me. I didn't know if I was forcing them to or if it was of their own free will. It didn't matter, as long as in the end, they understood.

"This has to remain a secret, obviously." I chuckled. "It's only you guys who know. It has to stay that way. You know that I count on you. You're my best friends." *How could they resist that plea?* They couldn't. They didn't. We all swore a pact, then and there. My secret was safe.

Jonathan perked up. "Hey, the deflated football. Oh, I get it now. What else can you do?"

I laughed. It was nice to do so. "I don't know, bruh. I haven't yet found out everything about this thing, this curse."

"Curse! Ha, more like superpowers," Jonathan exclaimed. Of course Jonathan hadn't thought about the bloodthirst part yet.

Junie added, "See like a cat in the dark, that's what you can do."

I pointed to my eyes. They all nodded their heads. "Yeah, evidently, I have, like…panther vision."

We went on to discuss the things that I knew I could already do, things that I might be able to do and things that we could experiment with, especially things we could use on James and the boys.

"Hey, but wait, have you used mind control on us? Have you read our minds?" Callie asked as she gave me the evil eye.

"Um, no!" I lied, sort of. Mostly I hadn't.

Jonathan then, with an inquisitive look, added, "Yeah, Michael, you have to promise, no mind tricks on us. You can't do that stuff on your friends...like not allowed!"

I laughed. "Yeah, yeah. Okay, I won't."

"No, promise it!"

"All right, I promise!" I meant it too. I didn't want to control my friends or read their thoughts. That was way too creepy.

We talked of many vampire issues on the way out of the forest. Naturally, I had to debunk all the myths, just as Drakon had done with me. I told them the old stories too, the stories of the Nosferatu, of Vlad. I told them of my blood thirst and that I only searched out the evil souls to feast upon. Somehow, to my surprise, they thought that was cool. *Freaks.* I did, however, leave Drakon—Mr. Branikov—out of the discussion. I figured his secret wasn't mine to tell.

As we were nearing the forest's edge, Callie stopped us. A thought had apparently come to her amid all this new vampire discussion. "What are you going to tell Hadley?"

Crap! I had forgotten about that.

"I don't know. Any ideas?" I looked at my friends. *Come on. You're supposed to be the geniuses. Give me something here.*

They were all thinking about it, but they all came up with nothing—nothing but a bunch of useless shrugs. I didn't have any idea what I was going to do. I wanted to tell Hadley that her father was dead. I thought she had the right to know. I just didn't want to tell her that I was the one who had caused it.

I finally decided that I would provide her with proof of her father's death, but I would twist the story of just how he met his demise.

My friends all wanted more time and had so many questions. They had become fascinated with my new but old-world gift. I had never been more popular within the group. However, it was getting late, so we had to go our separate ways.

Chapter Fifteen

Lies All Around

I got to Hadley's shack early the next morning. I wanted to spend some time with her before school started. I figured I could at least walk with her to school. I went out of my way and picked up some Sausage McMuffins with Eggs at McDonald's. I wasn't sure what Hadley and Lily's food supply was like, especially now with their dad missing.

I had a wad of money still from the saxophone sale. It was practically burning a hole in my pocket. I needed to find out how I could pay for Hadley's rent without pissing her off.

Creeuuuuk! The front porch steps gave me away again as I walked to the front door. *Dang, I'm going to have to fix these steps someday.* Lily, like usual, had the door open before I could even knock.

"It's Michael! Michael's here again! Did you bring anything?"

I gave Lily an ornery grin. I had the McDonald's bag hidden behind my back.

"What do you have? What's that?" Lily was trying to pull on my arm.

I finally caved, laughing. I handed her the bag. "Here ya go. Hey, share with your sister." I hollered as Lily started to run off. "Hello?" I peeked into the shanty.

"Come in," Hadley said, as she was standing in the small kitchen, apparently cleaning up.

Lily had jumped up onto a kitchen chair. She had already dumped out the contents of the McDonald's bag onto the table. Lily was not wasting any time. I smiled at Hadley and motioned for her to join. I had brought enough for all of us.

"Michael, you can't keep doing this," Hadley said, but then she reached in for a McMuffin.

I chuckled. "Ah, it's nothing. I have some extra money right now—and besides, I wanted some company." I gave Lily a wink. She giggled.

"Um, heard from your dad yet?" I asked, knowing full well that she had not.

Hadley looked at me then over to Lily. She used her mouth being full as an excuse to not say anything. She gave me a little head-shake no. I understood.

Dang, maybe I will wait until after school to tell her about her dad. I easily talked myself out of telling her. I was stalling.

I quickly changed the subject and asked Hadley about our English Lit assignment. I think she appreciated talking about something else, especially with Lily sitting there.

We walked Lily to her school then went around to the high school. That was when Hadley opened up a bit. "I didn't want to say anything with Lily around. She just thinks Dad is off on a work assignment. I lied to her. I didn't know what else to say right now but, Michael, I don't know. I think something has gone really wrong with him."

I looked at Hadley. A tear rolled down her cheek.

Oh shit, I have to tell her.

"Crap," I mumbled.

"What?" Hadley stopped on the sidewalk. I didn't know what to say. I slowly pulled out the photo I had been keeping in my pocket of Hadley, Lily and their dad.

Hadley recognized it right away. She snatched it from my hand. "Where did you get this?"

Now the lies would start. I told her that as I was leaving the gym, I'd heard two men in the side alley talking. I'd paused at the building's edge to listen.

I went on to tell Hadley more of the fabricated story. I told her that I could tell the men were a couple of drunks. They had been talking about a man who they had robbed at Shanty Town. I'd figured that it might have been her dad.

After hearing enough, I'd decided to jump out from the building and confront the drunks. I'd figured that since it was broad daylight, what would they do? Well, I'd startled them so badly in their drunken state that they'd run.

One man had dropped a small paper bag that he was carrying. He'd tried to go back for it, but then he'd seen me and kept running. I'd thought they were scared. I told her that I'd thought they might have done something really bad to her dad and that they didn't want me to see their faces. *Geez, what a whopper of a story.*

I told Hadley what I'd found in the paper bag. *More lies!* I pulled out the rest of the papers that had been in her dad's wallet. I showed her the license. Hadley began to cry. Naturally, I just held her. I let her sob into my shoulder. I didn't know what else to do.

Finally, after she calmed down and she'd stood back a little. I gently wiped the tears from her cheek.

"But wait, Hadley, there's something good." I had one thousand dollars of my saxophone sale, minus the McDonald's purchase, rolled up in a rubber band. It had been safely stuffed in my pocket. I had been waiting for a moment like this. "This was in the bag. I think your dad was coming home with the rent money. I think that maybe he was killed for it." I held out the wad of money in front of Hadley.

She looked down at it, almost crying again.

"Please, take it. It's yours, for rent," I said.

Hadley gingerly took the money out of my hand. She looked into my eyes in a way that made my heart pound. I felt something that I had never felt before. Then her soft lips touched mine, taking my breath away. I reached out to hold her. I wanted to hold her forever, but she quickly pulled away, distancing herself from my reach.

What followed was an awkward moment. To ease both our suffering, I grinned. "Come on. We're going to be late for school."

Hadley stuffed the wad of money into her pocket and we headed down the sidewalk, discussing schoolwork like nothing had happened.

We went our separate ways when school started. I was on a cloud all morning, reliving that moment. I wondered if it had also been special for Hadley.

Third period rolled around. I'd found Hadley sitting in the back of the classroom and had sat down at the desk next to her. As class started, I'd tried to get a sense for what she was thinking. I didn't want to just outright read her mind. That would have only made me feel guilty and possibly would have had repercussions of learning about some sad thoughts that I didn't really want to know.

I sat there thinking about Hadley, the kiss and the bracelet that was burning a hole in my pocket, and I was still trying to listen to Mrs. V. Somebody kicked my foot. *Oh.* I awoke from my trance and looked over at Hadley. She was trying to slide me a note.

I quickly grabbed it when Mrs. V looked away, placing it within my lit book so that I could read it without being suspicious.

Michael,

Thanks so much for finding my dad's stuff. I can't believe there was that much money. Dad never made that much in a month. It makes me wonder what he was up to. But anyway, it is enough money to pay for 2 months' rent, with almost $200 left over. You sure you didn't have anything to do with this? Most people that I've known in my life would have kept this money for themselves, and yet you gave it all to me. Wow!

Don't tell anyone! I, like you, now think Dad is dead. I knew this was coming. He had been having troubles for so long. I tried to prepare myself, but it's still hard. However, if anyone finds out, they will take Lily away, so you have to keep my secret. Thank you again. I'm so glad we are friends.

P.S. You could come with me to pay the rent? I'm a little afraid of the landlord. He's kind of a scumdog.

What? Glad we are friends. Dang! I'd been hoping for more than that, but still, there was an invitation to help her with something further. Most certainly I was in.

I folded the note and put it in my pocket. I looked over at Hadley and gave her a thumbs-up from behind my lit book.

Chapter Sixteen

Phlebotomy Lab Heist

The first thing my friends wanted to discuss at lunch were my new abilities.

"Dang, guys, Hadley doesn't know. If she joins us, you have to shut it," I whispered as I looked around to make sure no one was listening. Actually, no one ever listened to our table. I don't know why I was so paranoid.

"Really, you told us, but you haven't told her yet? Michael, you're such a dork sometimes," Callie said, shaking her head at me.

Junie nudged Jonathan. "Ask him," she whispered.

Like I didn't hear her, really? "Ask me what?"

Jonathan fiddled around with his pizza, stalling, then he asked, "Um, can we have a sample of your blood? You know, like, to test? For, like...a science experiment?"

"What?" Even though I questioned Jonathan out loud, I had been thinking about my blood—a blood test, to be exact. This was actually good timing. My doctor's appointment was coming up and Dr. Yu always ran a blood test because of the testosterone that I took. I had been worrying that my new change—and not my F2M change, but my other change—might cause an issue with my blood test. I had been meaning to talk with Drakon about it, but maybe I could let Jonathan and Junie have a go at it.

"Which one of you knows how to take a blood sample?"

"Um, well, I have been reading up on how to do it," Junie replied.

Hadley walked up to the table. "How to do what?" she asked as she sat down with a piece of pizza. *Only one piece. Nothing else.* I could see she was watching her spending. She seemed so proud to be able to join us with her own plate of food. I found it interesting that something that simple made me feel happy.

Junie looked up at Hadley. Naturally, she had to lie. "Oh, we're studying blood in AP Biology. We're trying to talk Michael into donating some of his blood for our study."

Hadley laughed. "Oh, cool. Come on, Michael. A good friend would give them all the blood they needed."

"Grrr." I growled and shook my head. "I guess I will—but geez, let's get someone who knows how to take a blood sample properly. Don't ya think that would be a good idea?"

"Oh really? How hard can it be?" Junie replied. Then of course, everyone laughed—except me, that is. They found it funny. I wasn't so sure.

So the scheming began. We devised a plan for a phlebotomy lab heist. *All this talk about blood is starting to increase my thirst, dang it.*

Come to find out, Hadley was in the know when it came to blood. Evidently, since she'd turned sixteen, her dad had started taking her to the local phlebotomy lab. If she donated blood, they could get money. Because she was only sixteen, her dad had to initially sign a consent form, but now she was good to go. However, she could only go in every fifty-six days.

"But, guys, I think that was up like a week ago. I was going to go in anyway, you know, to earn some extra money. There's lots of blood lab equipment around there."

Junie and Jonathan perked up.

"So, like everything we need to get a sample of blood is there?" Junie asked.

"Oh yeah. No problem."

After a little more research and scheming, Junie and Jonathan came up with a plan.

Junie and Callie would go in with Hadley to the phlebotomy lab. They figured girls would be less suspicious and could get away with more. While Hadley was getting her blood drawn, Junie and Callie would need to get their hands on certain items — a tourniquet tube, alcohol wipes, a blood-tube holder and the needle used to draw the blood.

Jonathan and I would go into the office a few moments after their entry and cause some kind of distraction so that they could do all this without being noticed.

Great plan, right? Easy.

We decided to act on it the following day after school. There was no sense in wasting time. Otherwise, we might all chicken out. On the side, I also made plans with Hadley to help her pay her landlord. We would do that on Wednesday. She didn't want to wait. She told me that the deadline was Friday and that the landlord could be a real jerk about it.

Busy week. I needed to find an evening for myself. I needed to replenish my thirst. I had killed Hadley's dad, but it had been a waste — too much alcohol in his blood. I still needed to drink.

We all met after school at the usual place, by the baseball fields.

"We have to pick up Lily on the way." Hadley said right away.

"What? Won't that put a damper on our plans?" Jonathan asked.

"Nah, they know her there. Besides, she might help keep the lab techs distracted. They like to mess with Lily and give her attention. That might give us a better chance to get what we need."

Jonathan shrugged. "Okay, whatever you think, Hadley."

The rest of us agreed that it was okay. We had no idea what the blood lab was like. That was Hadley's deal. Plus, I knew Hadley had to pick up Lily. It wasn't like they had a parent around to go get her. What was I going to say? No? *Yeah, I don't think so.*

Jonathan and I stayed across the street while the girls entered the lab. We tried to act nonchalant and unsuspicious. We would go in to be a distraction when Callie texted me.

It only took about ten minutes for me to get a text. All it read was *Now!* I figured that it obviously meant we were up. However, Jonathan and I didn't really have a plan. I didn't know what we were going to do. We were just going to wing it.

We waltzed into the front doors of the lab. Certainly, it was a slow day. Only a few sad-looking people were sitting in the small lobby area.

Jonathan gave me a look like, "What do we do?"

Oh geez, this was poorly planned. I chuckled then shrugged. Clueless.

We both walked up to the front desk. A young lady looked up from behind the counter. "May I help you boys?"

"Um…" Thank goodness Lily spotted me from across the room. She came running up. "Michael! Michael!"

I figured this was as good a chance as any to make a distraction. I met Lily halfway across the lab floor. I picked her up with ease and threw her over my shoulder. I began to spin in circles, like someone would do when they goofed off with little kids.

It couldn't have been more perfect. Lily's feet swung out. I spun over to the side on purpose. In an instant we got tangled in a patron's tubing. The blood bag pulled away and landed on the floor. Disaster followed. It was great!

Blood splattered everywhere. The floor became a large red mess. I still had Lily on my shoulder. She somehow found the whole thing funny and was giggling. The lab techs, on the other hand, were yelling at me. However, they had become a blur in the background. I found myself focused on the blood.

I put Lily down. I almost wanted to get down on my hands and knees and lap the blood up off the floor. It looked so appetizing. My head began to swirl.

I picked up the open end of the patron's blood tube. In a haze, I think I was about ready to stick the tube in my mouth and suck out the blood.

I felt a hand clench my arm. "Come on, Michael. We need to get out of here." It was Callie's voice.

I shook my head a little, turned and looked to see a worried face. Callie tilted her head toward the door.

"Yes, yes! You get out of here now!" a lab tech yelled at me.

I turned to look back at Hadley. *Did she see me do anything strange?* I wasn't sure what I had done. Hadley was just shaking her head, but then she gave me an eye roll. I figured then that I was okay. I must have just made a mess of things. *Okay, maybe I overdid the distraction part a little bit, but hopefully the girls got what we came for.*

Jonathan, Callie and I exited in a rush, with Callie still dragging me by my arm.

"Well, did you get what we needed?" I asked as we got out onto the sidewalk and I pulled my arm away from Callie's grip, giving her a frown.

"Geez, Michael, overdo the distraction thing a little? And dang, were you going to like drink the blood or what?"

She and Jonathan just stared at me, waiting for an answer. I shrugged. "I don't know...maybe."

They shook their heads then just laughed. I don't know why they found that so funny. I didn't. The feeling of needing to replenish and coming so close but then being pulled away left me feeling so very empty — not hungry but unfulfilled.

Trying to put the whole blood-spill out of my mind, I focused on the items Callie was now pulling out of her jacket pockets. She had a few we were going to need, but not near everything.

"What? That's not going to work!"

"Duh, Junie has the rest, you dork. You think I could like fit everything in my pockets?" Callie smarted off.

I guess that should have been obvious. I was curious about my blood and what a test might show, yet in the back of my mind I was hoping this caper would fail. I wasn't quite sure that I wanted Junie poking a needle into my arm.

It wasn't more than another fifteen minutes or so and Junie, Hadley and Lily came walking out of the door. We all headed down the street to a little corner park where we would be able to take a look at the items without being bothered.

Hadley and Junie were still laughing about the whole debacle. Little Lily was puzzled by our conversation along the way, but she was no fool. "Michael, did you swing me into that guy in the lab on purpose? You wanted to make a mess?"

I looked down at Lily, surprised by her brilliance. I laughed. "Well, I didn't mean to cause that much of a mess."

"What are you guys all up to?" Lily asked as she stopped and put her hands on her hips.

"Um, school stuff, Lily," Hadley answered.

"Yeah, right. I'm going to tell Dad."

Hadley looked over to me, not knowing what to say.

"Hey, Lily, you know that tomorrow I'm going to be around again. Maybe we can do some ice cream." I knew just bringing that word up would distract Lily. It did.

While we kept Lily talking about ice cream, Junie and Callie spread out the heisted blood lab items on a park bench. I had no idea if we had what we needed. They looked like a bunch of foreign items to me. I didn't like the look of the big-ass needle.

We decided to do the dirty deed — the blood draw — at Hadley's place. There would be no parents at home. She, of course, told everyone that her dad was off working. I knew better — and so did they, but my friends covered well.

I was surprised that Hadley wasn't embarrassed to have everyone over to her little shanty. However, it didn't seem to bother her. I guess she figured we all knew that she was poor, so why hide it. Plus, her shanty was kind of cute, and she did keep it clean inside.

Junie and Jonathan offered to buy McDonald's on the way there. Everybody jumped at the offer. Lily was pleased to get a Happy Meal.

We got settled in at Hadley's. Junie spread out all the equipment on the coffee table. They had me sit on the couch. Junie started inspecting the veins in my arm. She was not looking so good. Her face was getting pale.

"Are you sure you can do this?" I asked as Junie reached for the tourniquet tubing.

"Um, no problem. Well, I studied how to do this a lot anyway."

"Oh geez," I mumbled.

Junie fumbled around. I could tell she was stalling. She finally wiped down hopefully the right spot with an alcohol wipe. She was getting ready to put the needle into the vein. However, things didn't go so well. Her hand started to tremble. Her face got clammy and pale. She began to sway.

Down onto the floor Junie went. Fainted. *Yeah, Junie isn't going to be able to draw my blood sample.*

Everybody else was laughing. Not me. This was a disaster. I must have had a terrified look on my face.

Hadley stepped forward. "No worries, Michael. I can do this. I've had this done on me so many times. It's a piece of cake."

Junie sat back up and handed Hadley the needle. Luckily it was still okay. As Junie wiped off her face, she said, "Yeah, Hadley, you best do this."

Hadley chuckled. She cleaned off the needle with one of the alcohol wipes. "I got this."

Hadley managed to do everything like it was nothing new, like a pro. It didn't even hurt that much. She succeeded in filling up the sample tube with my blood. Now Junie and Jonathan would have plenty of blood to experiment with.

What will it show?

Chapter Seventeen

Scum-Dog Landlord

I met up with Hadley after school the next day. It was time to go pay her landlord. First we had to pick up Lily. I had made her a promise the day before that I would get her some ice cream. *Did I think she would forget? Ha.*

As soon as her school bell rang, Lily ran out of the door. "Michael! Michael, are you taking me for ice cream?"

"Dang, girl, I'm fine. My day has been good, and how are you?"

Lily giggled.

Luckily, I had brought some extra money along. I still had another thousand dollars left from the saxophone sale.

"Come on." I looked at Hadley. "Ice cream first, then the rent?"

Hadley sighed and shook her head, but then as Lily looked at her with those big blue eyes, Hadley caved. "All right."

After some delicious cookies-and-cream ice cream and a bit of fun messing with Lily, which she loved, we headed off to the landlord's office. Mr. McDouglas was his name and he owned McDouglas Rental Properties. His office was in my favorite part of town. Not really… It was in the slummy area, the scum-dog area, the place where I'd killed my first victim. *Nice!*

I didn't want to say anything with Lily standing right there as we walked up to the office. I pointed to the adult Déjà Vu Love store right next door. Hadley gave me an elbow and glanced down at Lily. I smirked.

As we walked into the small, grungy, rundown office, a rough and unshaven older looking man looked up from a single desk that sat near the back wall. "Hello. You kids lost? I'm busy," the man, presumably Mr. McDouglas, said in a very abrupt tone.

It looked like he was working on some kind of accounting books. He took a second glance up at us, peering over his reading glasses. "Oh, it's you. Where's your dad? You know your rent is about due?"

Hadley paused. I could tell she was nervous. I gently held her hand, just to let her know that I was there to back her up. She squeezed. *Dang, she has a strong grip for such a scrawny thing.* I was going to moan, but I held back and smiled instead, because I knew at that moment she needed me.

"Um, Dad sent me to pay our rent this month — and next month's too."

This time the man definitely took notice. He took off his reading glasses, placed them on the desk and suddenly sat straight up in his chair.

"He did, did he? Hmm, well, how much money you got?"

I sensed something wrong right away. He was up to no good. I figured now was a good time to do some mind reading.

What a joke this is. Jake thinks he can send in his little girl to do his bidding. What is he trying to pull? Well, watch this. I'll take advantage of his little scheme. No one gets one over on me.

Hadley was reaching for her money. I quickly grabbed her hand and shook my head no. She stopped and gave me a puzzled look. I stepped forward, put my hands down on the desk and leaned in toward Mr. McDouglas. "Uh-hm, so how much is two months' rent for the Johnsons? And we will need a receipt if we pay upfront," I said in a very stern voice.

Mr. McDouglas looked at me, then he laughed. "Who are you?"

"I'm a friend!"

"Well, it's four hundred a month, so eight hundred—but Hadley's dad was way behind on rent, so she owes me more just to catch up."

I concentrated on his thoughts.

I will take her for all the money she has. She'll never know that her dad didn't owe me anything. How easy this will be.

"Bullshit!"

Hadley looked at me. Lily giggled then whispered, "Michael said a bad word."

I looked down at Lily, smiled and gave her a wink, but then I looked back to Mr. McDouglas and glared viciously.

"Hadley will pay two months' rent, you will give her a discount for paying in advance and you will write out a receipt so that she has proof." I hoped my Obi-Wan mind trick would work.

The dirtbag of a man paused, looked at us, shook his head and then said, "Okay, Ms. Hadley. I'm not sure why, but if you pay now for two months, I will only charge you six hundred dollars and I will give you your receipt."

Hadley quickly paid Mr. McDouglas, got the receipt and we hurried out of the door, before the scum-dog slumlord changed his mind. *Hmm, next victim, maybe? What a jerk!* And tonight I needed to go out. I couldn't put it off any longer.

Hadley was elated. She now had four hundred dollars left over. She and Lily could stock up on some groceries for a change. Even Lily was excited. However, Lily did ask one question.

"When is Dad coming home?"

Chapter Eighteen

Slumlord for Dinner and Blood Test Results

Hadley had to break down and tell Lily that their dad likely wouldn't be coming home. She didn't tell Lily that he was dead. She just told her that he was gone…and for a long time.

Lily didn't really get it, but she finally accepted what Hadley told her. She wasn't happy about the situation, but she agreed to go on with the way things were. She kept it a secret because Hadley convinced her that she could be taken away if anyone found out that their dad was gone.

Lily asked Hadley if I could move in with them. She told Hadley that it would make everything okay. That filled me with arrogance. Really, I was pretty overwhelmed that little Lily was so strongly attached to me already. I was hoping this might make Hadley appreciate me even more. I could only hope. Of course, Hadley and I just laughed at the idea, but it was cute of Lily to think of us being together.

Late that afternoon, I left Hadley and Lily. I didn't go right home. Blood. I needed to quench my thirst and I knew just who was on my list.

I made my way to the McDouglas Rental Property office. My hope was that Mr. McDouglas would still be there.

A soft white light was flickering through the window shades from the office building. I could sense that a human was nearby. I scanned around the area. There were a few street urchins over on the corner, but that wasn't what I was sensing. Mr. McDouglas was still here.

There was no car parked out front. He must use a back entrance. That was better for me anyway. I walked up to the street corner then around to the alley, trying to avoid being seen by anyone.

Behind the office sat a black Mercedes-Benz. Some kind of sporty coupe. It was pretty sick. *Figures.* I peeked in the windows. Cushy leather seats too. The dude obviously had some money and he flaunted it too. *Slumlords, ha!* They own a bunch of divey properties that need all kinds of work. Heaven forbid they spend any of their money to fix up the places. No, let their renters live in squalor.

This was me, trying to give myself a good reason to feast on this man. He'd already tried to rip off Hadley. Did I need any more of a reason? Well, kind of. More would be better.

The back door opened as I was standing there trying to persuade myself. Mr. McDouglas stepped out and jumped as he saw me. "What the hell, kid? Oh, you were the one here earlier today, with that Hadley girl. What are you doing back here?"

"Why were you lying to Hadley?"

Mr. McDouglas just stood there, silent in the open door.

"Why did you try and swindle her out of more rent money than what she really owed?"

He laughed. "What do you know, kid? What do you think you're going to do about it anyway? Go home and mind your own business!"

"How many poor people do you take advantage of?"

The jerk started to walk away, chuckling to himself. I read his mind. *All that I can. All that I can.* He was still chuckling as he brushed me aside.

I knew now that he fit my mandatory checklist. Loser, and he was an asshole. *Hmm, what else?* He obviously cared little for anyone else, and most of all, I sensed he had an evil soul. I needed nothing more. I attacked as he turned his back on me like I was nothing.

My arm went across his neck, like an MMA wrestler putting on a chokehold. I easily threw the man down onto the ground like a rag doll. I swung around and was on top of him before he knew what was going on. I used so much force that I think I may have broken his neck. No matter, the feast began.

I was more careful and in control this time. The blood splatter was much less of a problem. I wiped my face off on the man's jacket, keeping my own shirt clean—or at least cleaner. As I looked down, with only the alley light, my keen night vision picked up only a few spots of blood on my shirt. I was extremely proud of myself. I chuckled a bit, finding it funny.

Oh man, did I feel good…on top of the world again. I stood up and over the man, like a proud lion over his kill, relishing the moment. It wasn't long, though, until

I glanced down and the harsh reality settled back in. It was body removal time.

I wish I could drive. Driver's Ed wasn't until next semester. *Dang!* I had driven an old pickup truck a couple of times out on my uncle's farm. I was tempted as I looked at the nice Mercedes. Nope, it would be a disaster if I tried to take the body away in the car. I decided that I'd best stick to Drakon's routine. This body would go to the dark and dank crevasse.

First, I remembered to search the man for money. He had a little. However, I noticed he had been carrying a briefcase. I tried to open it. Locked. I didn't have time to mess with it now, so I decided to keep it. I would check it out later.

I got rid of the body with no issues. I could carry the man over one shoulder and the briefcase in the other hand. It was like a walk in the park. I was getting stronger — or maybe it was because I had just replenished. Either way, it was pretty savage!

No problems. Home in time for supper. I ran upstairs first, cleaned up a bit and changed clothes. I threw the briefcase onto my desk. I would deal with that later.

I meandered back downstairs, cool and calm. Smells of fried chicken filled the air. *Heavenly.* Mom was such a good cook. I was amazed that even though I had just feasted, I still found myself wanting a piece of fried chicken.

"Busy today? Sit down and take a break for a bit, sweetie."

I smiled at Mom. She always knew the right thing to say. I plopped down in the chair. Suddenly all my cares and worries were gone.

Supper at my house was a pleasant time. Mom, Dad and I could sit down, enjoy some good food and have a nice conversation. There were no invading questions and no judgements, just casual, peaceful family talk.

I finished up, helped Mom with the dishes then told her I had homework, which was a true statement.

The briefcase sat on my desktop. I fiddled with it for a bit. I could just break it with my super strength, but I didn't want to damage anything that was inside. *What if it's holding something really valuable and fragile? Or explosives? Yeah, doubtful.* I laughed at my own ridiculous thoughts. I fiddled with the case for a little while longer, but then slid it aside after getting frustrated. I needed to do my homework anyway.

Some math first. Then I pulled out my English lit book that we were supposed to be reading, *The Catcher in the Rye*. Not for me. I would rather be reading some fantasy or sci-fi book, but I didn't get a choice in the matter.

Rather than sit at my desk, I got comfortable on my bed and started reading the required two chapters.

Beep, beep, beep, beep! My morning alarm was sounding. *Crap!* I was still in my clothes from the previous night and had an open book lying on my chest. I must have really been tired. I quickly scurried out of bed, showered, put on clean clothes, rushed around some more and almost combed my hair. I didn't ever give myself much time from when my alarm went off to when I had to be out of the door. I didn't need it, but I was usually a little more organized from the night before. Not this time.

I glanced at the briefcase – *later* – and grabbed the rest of my books, then ran down to the kitchen. Mom tossed me a banana, as she saw I was rushing. Really, I just wanted to meet Hadley to walk with her and Lily to school.

"Later," I hollered as I ran out of the door.

* * * *

Lunchtime came around quickly. Everybody was at our usual table. Hadley was once again proudly sporting her own piece of pizza—me, fries and an apple. It just didn't get any better than that.

"So, um…we've been working on your blood sample," Jonathan said as he looked at Junie then back to me with an unsure stare.

"What?" I asked, "Come on. Tell me. What did you guys find out?"

Junie nudged Jonathan and whispered, "Tell him."

"Tell me *what*?" I frowned and glared at both my friends.

Jonathan kind of gave a side glance to Hadley. "Um, later. We're still finalizing the results."

That's right. Hadley doesn't know my secret yet. Oops, almost slipped up.

Callie was quick to catch on. She changed the subject immediately. Luckily, Hadley was enjoying her pizza too much and missed the gist of the conversation. I chuckled. "That good?" Hadley just nodded as she had her mouth full. We all laughed at her. She was clueless but seemed to be happy with whatever—happy, I think, just to have something to eat for lunch.

James and the boys walked by. Funny… They stayed a long way off, sitting at a table clear across the room. Lunch ended up being pretty dang peaceful for a change. I did give them a wave on our way out. I had to torment them a little bit.

The rest of the day drove me crazy. All I could think about was what Junie and Jonathan might have found. I didn't have any of the same classes, so I would have to track them down at the library after school.

Instead of jogging to the gym, I headed over to the dreaded library, a place I normally avoided. I found Junie, Jonathan and Callie sitting at their usual table. I was always amazed that these guys didn't get their fill at school. They have to come spend another couple of hours studying here.

I shook my head as I approached them and chuckled. *Geeks for sure.* I casually sat down in the empty chair at the table. "What's up?"

They all looked up from their textbooks like I was a thing of annoyance.

"Well?" I questioned Jonathan and Junie right away. I had been waiting all day to find out about my blood tests.

Finally, Jonathan closed his textbook. Junie and Callie proceeded to do the same. They all stared at me, purposely torturing me.

"Dang, that bad?" I asked as I looked at each of my friends for any kind of clue.

"Um, kind of… Going by what we've studied so far, bruh, this is so lit!" Jonathan said as he started to show some excitement.

"And?" I asked as I sighed. *Like…come on already.*

Jonathan went on to explain, and I think he did so without even taking a breath, like an excited little kid telling a story. He told me that they were studying my blood on slides under a microscope in the AP Science Lab. All on the sly, of course.

"Extraordinary!" Jonathan exclaimed in the middle of his explanation.

He went on to tell me that it appeared as though some of my red blood cells were abnormal. His words, "very abnormal blood indeed." He told me that it appeared as if these abnormal cells were demolishing — or as Jonathan put it, 'eating' — my normal blood cells. He described it as a virus, a viral blood cell that was absorbing any normal blood cell.

"This must be the virus you told us about. You know, the one from your story caused by the Black Viper bite. This virus is what is making you need...um, well, to drink blood."

I sat back in my chair. It made sense. After thinking about it for a moment and with everybody awkwardly staring at me, I asked Jonathan, "Can you and Junie cure it?"

Laugher broke out. We got a 'shush' from the librarian.

"No, seriously," I whispered.

"Yeah, bruh, seriously? Do we look like epidemiologists?"

"Um, like *what*?"

"Do we look like medical doctors that study in the field of diseases?"

I paused, looked my friends over. "Um, well, yeah?" I chuckled.

Everybody laughed, quietly this time. Callie even agreed with me on that one, as she was nodding.

"Okay already, Mr. Epidemi-whatever-scientist dude, can you guys cure it for real?"

Jonathan and Junie looked at me and shook their heads.

"Bro, like I said, No! There's like not a chance. This is well beyond Junie and me."

"Damn," I mumbled. Although part of me wasn't too sure that I wanted to be cured. Some of what went along with this curse or virus, I kind of liked.

"So who did you get this virus from anyway? It's not like there are any Black Vipers around here. Who was the one who passed this onto you?" Jonathan asked.

"Yeah, who?" Callie also asked.

"Dracula?" Junie blurted out.

I chuckled. "No." *Although, I don't think Drakon is too far distant a relative.*

"Well, who, then?" Callie probed.

"Ha! You guys know that I can't tell you. That would be betrayal on my part. Sorry, guys. That has to remain a secret."

"Dang, Michael, you suck," Jonathan said in protest. However, I knew he understood.

I shrugged. There was not much else to say.

"Oh yeah, one more question, Michael. Does blood type matter? I mean, you're probably O-positive, so can you drink like any type of blood."

"Hmm, good question. I don't know for sure. I guess I'll find out if I ever get the wrong blood type." I hadn't thought of that. *Dang, maybe it's a good thing most people are O-positive. I wonder what happens if I drink like an AB negative person's blood?*

I found all this new information interesting. No wonder I needed to replenish my blood every so often. However, now I needed to ask the important question and hopefully my smart friends would know the answer.

"Okay, Jonathan or Junie, when I go in to get my bloodwork done for my testosterone level check, is the doctor going to find out about all of this?"

Jonathan looked to Junie, then to me. He shrugged.

Junie finally spoke out. "You'll be okay, Michael. I don't believe they will be looking at your blood under a microscope. I expect they are just going to measure the testosterone levels. Um, I don't think they will find anything."

By the way Junie's voice sounded, I could tell she wasn't completely sure, but I would have to hope she was right.

Chapter Nineteen

Money, Money, Money

My doctor's appointment with Dr. Yu went well. It made me nervous when the technician took my blood sample. All I could imagine was a vicious battle of blood cells. Creepy. Hopefully the T test would go well. I tried not to think about it, like that was working.

I talked with Dr. Yu about furthering my transition. I was ready to finish my F2M transition completely. He educated me about what it would take to complete the bottom half. It didn't sound pleasant—kind of horrifying—but I was so ready to make the sacrifice. I really wanted a complete body for Michael.

Dr. Yu said he would talk more with my parents about the issue. However, I knew the main problem right now was insurance coverage and money. Mom and Dad had already sacrificed so much for me. I hated to push the issue. I told Dr. Yu to hold off for the time being.

I got my blood test back. All that worry had been for nothing. Everything was supposedly okay. It made me laugh. *Yeah, if they only knew.* It was definitely a relief, though. One less thing to worry about.

I had been busy all week. I'd almost forgotten about the briefcase that was sitting at the back of my desk. On Saturday morning, I finally took notice.

After sleeping in an extra hour—okay, maybe two—I slowly woke up. I was sitting on the edge of my bed, thinking about what I wanted to do that day. I was also thinking about how I could make up an excuse to go see Hadley. The edge of the briefcase caught my eye. *Oh shit! I almost forgot about you. Time to see what treasures you hold.*

I tossed the case onto my bed and sat down alongside it. *Wait, breakfast first, or Mom will be knocking on my door, wondering what's up.* I quickly ran downstairs, still in my pajamas, which was typical for a Saturday morning. I grabbed an orange juice and started to take it back upstairs.

"Whoa! Leaving so quickly? Michael, sit down for a minute. I've hardly seen you all week. Tell me about school. Tell me more about this Hadley girl. Plus, I made blueberry muffins."

Dang, Mom—the briefcase was calling to me, but how could I refuse a blueberry muffin just out of the oven?

I decided to sit down at the kitchen table for just a moment. Mom handed me a muffin on a plate. The butter was melting over the top of it just the way I liked. It did smell delicious.

Mom and I talked—a little about school, mostly about Hadley. She knew that I kind of liked the girl.

It was actually a pretty nice talk. Mom knew how to give me advice without seeming like she was doing so. I don't know how she did that, but she was good at it.

Geez, an hour had passed before I knew it. "Mom, I've got things to do today. Later. Oh, and thanks for the muffin." I gave her a thumbs up as I got up to leave the kitchen.

As I was walking up the stairs, I heard her say, "Tell Hadley I said hello."

I shook my head and chuckled. "Oh, Mom," I mumbled.

Now, back to the briefcase. It had a combination lock on the front. I messed with that for a while. *Forget it.* How many number combinations could there be? Too many.

Finally, I decided on force. I got a screwdriver from the garage. I tried prying it between the seams of the case but it wouldn't fit. *Dang, this is one tough briefcase.* Deciding that the case probably wasn't full of explosives, I settled on using my brute force. I jammed the screwdriver into the seam just above the lock. *Oops, a little too hard.* It went into the case up to its hilt. I had to wiggle it back out a little.

I pried and pried. *Pop!* The lock clasp gave way. Out flew pieces of paper, everywhere. *Wait, not pieces of paper! Money!* The case was full of money — hundred-dollar bills, to be exact. Stacks of them. *Wow! This guy was definitely a crook.* I wondered what Mr. McDouglas had been doing with all this money. When I'd attacked him that night outside his office, the banks would have been closed. *Hmm, where was he going with all this money? Maybe he has a big stash hidden somewhere?*

I quickly stuffed all the money back into the case and looked around, feeling guilty, like someone might be watching. *What a dork.* I was in my room alone. Somehow, it still made me really nervous.

I took one bundle of hundreds back out once I'd calmed down. The bundle had a paper band around it. I counted the bills. One, two, three, all the way to one hundred! *Dang. Let's see…* That made for ten thousand dollars a bundle. One, two…thirty bundles. Damn, three hundred thousand dollars!

On that thought, I slammed the top shut. My mind was spinning. *Is my math right?* I was a nervous wreck as I hid the case deep within the mess on my closet floor. It was doubtful anyone would ever find it there. I chuckled at my sloppiness. Then my mind went back to the amount of money. I asked again as I mumbled to myself, "Did I really figure that out right? Holy crap!"

I sat down on my bed, staring into my closet. My thoughts began to race. The things I could do with that money. I could do my bottom-half surgery. I could complete my transition. I imagined I would have enough money left over to even pay for college. The ideas swirled about in my mind like a whirlwind.

I had to tell someone. I was going to burst with excitement. *Head to Hadley's. But what kind of story would I tell her?* I wanted to share the news about the money, but I couldn't exactly tell her the truth.

I put on my workout clothes and told Mom that I was headed out for a bit. I'm sure she assumed that I was headed to the gym. I was not. Shanty Town was where I was headed.

"Jacket!" Mom hollered as I was about to go out of the door.

Oh crap, misty rain and fog. I hadn't even looked outside yet this morning in all my excitement. I grabbed my usual jacket and was out of the door. As I got closer to Shanty Town, the misty rain turned into a downpour. *Dang, I should have worn my waterproof jacket. Duh, dummy.*

I was soaked by the time I found myself on Hadley's front porch, really hoping she was home. Like usual, the steps gave out a loud creak. However, this time no one, not even Lily, met me at the door.

Hmm, maybe they aren't home. Hadley really needs to get a cell phone. Of course, when someone doesn't even have money for food, I guess a phone is the last thing on their list.

I knocked on the door. Nothing. I knocked a little harder. The door flew open, but nobody was there. Somebody had to have opened the door, but then they'd obviously left in a hurry.

"What do you want? We are a little busy here!" Hadley angrily yelled.

I stepped in to see what was up.

"Oh, it's you."

Geez, that's a fine welcome. "Hello?" I questioned, but then I saw the mess.

There were pots everywhere. Streams of water were coming in from a noticeably leaky roof. Lily and Hadley were frantically running back and forth to the kitchen sink, dumping pots of water then placing them back under any leak that looked bad. There were definitely too many for them to keep up with.

"Well, don't just stand there. Grab a pot!"

"Dang! Yeah, okay." I replied as I grabbed one pot that was already overflowing with water. Although I wasn't sure what the point was now — the floor was already a huge pool of water. I thought they would be better off pushing the water out with a broom, but I didn't want to say anything. Hadley wasn't exactly in a good mood at the moment.

As we were shuffling pots back and forth, I was messing around with Lily a bit. Hadley ended up yelling at us. I was just trying to make some fun of the whole debacle. However, at that moment, I started to feel a little bit guilty.

All that money and all I had thought about was how I could spend it on myself. I hadn't once thought about Hadley. *What kind of jerk am I?* She needed a new house — but how could a sixteen-year-old kid buy a house?

I needed Drakon's help. This was beyond my knowledge. *Hmm, thinking on this matter, will I be sixteen forever?* Another question for Drakon.

The rain finally eased off and the water downpours in the house came to slow drips. Lily, Hadley and I fell on the couch in complete exhaustion.

"Eww!" Lily screamed as she jumped up. She turned around to show us her rear end. It was soaked. We had missed a leak. That end of the couch had apparently been drenched. *Oops.* Hadley and I still managed to laugh, even amid the horror of the whole situation. Lily stomped off to the back room, I assumed to find a different pair of pants.

"Dang, Hadley, this is a mess."

Hadley looked at me and shook her head. "Oh, this is nothing. You should see it when it really rains."

My eyes widened. I couldn't imagine. Hadley broke out into laughter. I couldn't believe that she could still laugh about it all. I chuckled a little. "But…"

Hadley stopped me. "Oh, don't worry. It's just water. It will always dry out."

"Hmm." She did have a point, but I don't think I would be able to take it as well as she did. I definitely had to help her and Lily out now. I took my own house for granted. It was time Hadley had someplace nice to live. Besides, Shanty Town wasn't exactly a safe place to be either.

Hadley and I went on with sweeping out water, emptying pots and drying off what we could with a few hand towels. Lily came back crying.

"What now?" Hadley asked as she gave an eye roll.

"How come if Dad is gone on a trip, all of his clothes are still in the bedroom?"

Hadley looked at me. I shrugged. *Crap! Like I knew what to say.* Hadley paused, then finally said, "Um, I don't know, Lil. His work must have given him uniforms. Yeah, you know, they probably gave him work clothes." Hadley looked at me with a questionable questioning on her face. I almost laughed, but that wouldn't have been appropriate. Poor Lily.

Lily stood there, glaring at us both, looking back and forth to each of us, pondering her question and her sister's answer. Oh man, was my guilt really stirring inside now. *Yep, definitely have to get these two a house.*

Lily scowled. "Okay."

I know she was only five, but she was beginning to catch on. *Can I tell Hadley the truth?*

I still had part of the saxophone money left. I hadn't touched the briefcase money yet. So I took the girls to McDonald's for lunch. It was a much-needed break. Lily mostly played in the play area, which was good because it gave Hadley and me time alone.

It was nice just to relax and talk. I thought it ended up being a great conversation. We laughed a lot and it seemed that we were really connecting. I felt like I could be myself — well, almost myself.

Afterward, we parted ways. Hadley had to go to the laundromat. She and Lily were evidently running low on clean clothes. Hadley made Saturdays their day to do the wash.

I wasn't headed home yet. I needed to talk to someone…Drakon. He was probably home with his family, though. *How do I get a hold of him? I don't want to be too much of a bother. But hey, after all, he is the one who made me.*

I got about a block away from Drakon's house. I stood on the corner to see if there was any activity in his front yard. It looked pretty quiet.

Use my thoughts! *"Drakon, hello?"* Was I too far away? I know that the one night I was in trouble, he sensed it, and I was all the way in lower downtown.

I stood there like a creepy stalker, standing on the street corner alone, doing nothing, waiting.

"Yes?" Drakon's thoughts entered my mind. *"Do you need something?"*

"Um, are you like busy right now?"

I sensed a feeling of laughter from Drakon. *"No. Come on over to the house. I'll meet you on the front porch."*

I took my time. I wanted to give Drakon plenty of time. I didn't really know if I was interrupting his day. Hopefully not much was going on for him on a Saturday afternoon.

Drakon was sporting a pair of sweatpants. I almost laughed. He always looked so proper and older in school.

"What? You don't think I have a normal life outside of school?"

I shrugged and just grinned.

Drakon invited me to sit down on the porch swing with him. Mrs. Branikov peeked out of the front door. "You two want something to drink? Tea, lemonade?"

"Sure, dear, some lemonade for me. Michael?"

"Um, yeah, lemonade would be nice, thank you." I wondered how old Mrs. Branikov was. She looked to be much older than Drakon, looks-wise. Then I remembered that she would age and Drakon would not. I figured they must have been married quite some time already by her age.

"So, what's up?" Drakon interrupted my thoughts.

I went on to tell Drakon about my little run-in with Mr. McDouglas. I told him about everything, including the briefcase and the money.

"Ahh, it's about time somebody did in that slumlord. He was an evil soul for sure. I had also thought about taking him out once or twice before," Drakon said with a reassuring smile on his face. "You know, Michael, you might live a long time. The spoils of your decisions of whose lives you take can supplement your income. This may be needed in the long life that lies ahead of you."

I nodded. "But I'm only sixteen. What do I do with all this money — and, um, what if I want to like…buy a house?"

Drakon looked at me strangely. I went on to explain. I told him about Hadley and her situation.

"Oh, I see, the girl you have fallen in love with."

"Have not!"

Drakon laughed. Luckily, Mrs. Branikov came out about that time with our drinks and saved me from my anguish.

"Be nice, dear. He's just a lad." I heard her whisper to Drakon.

I gave him a raised eyebrow and nodded. We both chuckled once Mrs. Branikov had left. "She's a great woman, you know," Drakon said.

I could sense something sad about his statement. I looked at him for more details.

"She'll be turning forty-five this year. I know I dress and try to look like I am in my forties. My body is still only twenty-five...and yes, Michael, to answer the question that has been in the back of your mind, your body will still physically age. However, it will only age until you are fully developed, like your mid-twenties. Then, you will cease to age."

I looked at him with a questioning stare. "Like forever?"

"Yes...but you will learn how to deal with it, hide it. However, those you love will get old and you will lose many in the span of your life."

We both sat there in silence for a moment. Then Drakon patted me on the knee. "But love them each like they are the only one you have ever known. You'll never regret any of it. Now, back to the money issue."

It ended up that Drakon had a local banker friend — someone who was in the know, so to speak. Drakon's plan was to set me up with this banker guy after school on Monday. His name was Mr. Bill Green, and evidently he could set me up with a business and some sort of offshore banking account. I would run everything locally through an LLC. That way my name and age would be hidden.

Drakon told me that I would need such accounts to handle my assets in what would be a long life. Drakon was also interested in what Mr. McDouglas might have left behind.

Since I'd discarded the body properly and Mr. McDouglas apparently had no family in town, it was likely that he wouldn't be missed for days. Drakon suggested we investigate Mr. McDouglas further.

"So, if he had a briefcase full of money and the banks were closed, where do you think he was taking it?" Drakon questioned me.

Drakon and I went on to discuss the possibilities. We decided that we should investigate the man's house, and we should do so soon, before anyone noticed he was missing.

"Michael, this man was a slumlord and a lowlife. If he was hoarding money, we should make sure it does not fall into the wrong hands. That means we take it. We will put it to better use."

Somehow this felt like a moral dilemma for me. Drakon sensed this.

"Do you know of the soup kitchen on 4th Street?"

"Yes"

"That is my anonymous charity. Have you heard of the afterschool boys and girls club?"

"Yes."

"Also my charity, and yes, I have collected money for my own survival along the way. This is a long life. I have also taken money from many evil souls. However, I have created a way to give back to those who need it most, to those who it was most likely taken from to begin with."

I began to understand. Mr. McDouglas' money was from an evil source. If the police in this town confiscated it, it would either be taken by a corrupt cop or would waste away in an evidence locker. If Drakon and I took the money — if there was any — we could put it to better use, and since he was a slumlord, what better use than housing for some poor family?

Chapter Twenty

The Stash

First things first... Drakon and I set out for Mr. McDouglas' house that very night. Drakon did the recon. After sneaking out of my bedroom window, I met him at the corner of First Street and Illinois Avenue.

The nice thing about our small city was that it was pretty quiet in most neighborhoods at night, except for maybe the sleazy part of town, but we were surprisingly nowhere close to that. Mr. McDouglas, even though he was a slumlord, he didn't live in any slums. When I met up with Drakon, we were pretty close to the nicer part of the city.

Drakon wasted no time. "Follow me."

We stayed out of the streetlights, ducking in and out of alleyways and hanging near the hedges when possible. We came to the back of a tall wooden fence.

"Here. This should be the place."

Drakon tried the gate. It was locked. He could have easily broken it open, but before I could even say anything, Drakon leaped. One huge jump onto the top of the fence then over, like it was no big deal, graceful like a seasoned ballet dancer — and it was something like a six-foot fence.

The gate quickly opened from the other side. My mouth was still gaped open. Drakon laughed. "Come on. Time is a-wasting."

The house that stood before us was completely dark inside. Either no one was home or everyone was asleep. Drakon used a mind-probe trick. "No one is here. This is, in fact, Mr. McDouglas' house. I am sure."

It was a beautiful two-story house with brick exterior, big windows and an awesome courtyard in the back. *What a scum-dog! Owns a bunch of slum properties that he wouldn't spend a dime on fixing up and lives in a place like this*, I thought.

"Exactly!" Drakon replied.

I chuckled. I forgot that we were connected and he could read my thoughts.

We looked for an easy way in, but everything was locked up pretty tight. However, we both spotted a second-story window that looked to be slightly open.

I looked at Drakon. *I can't jump that high. Could he?* This was a lot higher than the fence.

Drakon just shook his head at me.

I was soon to get a lesson on another skill that I perhaps had and didn't realize, the ability to scale a wall. Drakon took off up the wall, holding on to the ever-so-small cracks between the mortar and the bricks. *Hmm, Spiderman skills.* Drakon reached the windowsill in no time at all. He went into the open window like a gymnast on rings, lifting his body up and through with grace and ease. I stood there and watched in awe.

In moments, Drakon was opening the back door.

"Well, you going to stand there all day? Come on in."

"Oh geez, that was like really quick." I said. I was utterly astonished.

I entered the back door. Even in the darkness, my keen vision could tell that we were in the kitchen. I went to flip on the light switch.

"Whoa, Michael! What are you doing? No lights!"

"Huh?"

Drakon's forehead furrowed. "Do you want the whole neighborhood to know we're here? Besides, use your night vision. It's by far good enough."

I looked around. He was right. I could see everything just fine. Actually, if I concentrated, I could see even the smallest details.

Drakon tapped me on the shoulder. He was shaking his head and laughing. I had obviously lost my train of thought for a moment. Drakon was holding out a pair of latex gloves in his hands. He had already put on a pair.

"We must be careful. We don't want to leave any evidence that we have been here. Now, let's go find the late Mr. McDouglas' stash. What do you say?"

"Oh yeah. We should look for a safe, ya think?"

"Hmm, indeed."

Drakon and I searched all the lower rooms, and there were a lot of them. Nothing found. Up the amazing wooden staircase we went. It was like something out of the movies, like that staircase in that old movie *Gone with the Wind*. Basically, the dude had lived in a mansion.

Bedroom after bedroom, but then we came to a big room that looked to be a study. It even had its own fireplace. *Dang, rich dudes suck.*

"Here!" Drakon proclaimed.

I felt it too. I knew, as did Drakon, that this was the room. Where else would a safe be hidden but behind a big-ass framed painting? It was a really well-done painting too. It was a sailboat down by a familiar seaside village that was not too far from here. I wondered if the boat in the painting was Mr. McDouglas' boat. *Anyway, back to the safe.*

Drakon pulled back the painting. There, within the wall, was a huge, heavy-duty-looking safe.

"How in the world are we going to get into that?" I asked as I stared at the huge beast of a thing.

Drakon laughed. "Not by force... How about a combination? A busy man such as Mr. McDouglas would have no doubt left himself a reminder somewhere around here."

We started searching. Drakon searched items on the fireplace mantle. I went to the desk. *Where would an arrogant asshole hide a combination?*

There was a framed Diamond Realtor award certificate. I didn't know what it was, but it was something Mr. McDouglas was certainly proud of. I carefully slid out the glass from the frame and pulled out the certificate. A yellow sticky note dropped out. Four numbers. That had to be it. I read them off to Drakon. "Two, sixty-five, twenty-four, sixty-five."

Click! The safe opened!

I was at Drakon's side before he opened the safe's door. I was as excited to see, as was Drakon, what was inside.

Stacks of money! Stacks of some kind of coins. "Gold and silver bullion," Drakon said.

There was also a stack of some kind of papers—I wasn't sure what they were yet—and lastly, a small velvet-covered case.

"What's up with the case?" I asked.

Drakon raised an eyebrow. "Oh, something good, I suspect."

He carefully opened the velvet case. Diamonds? Yes, the case was full of cut diamonds, like the kind in engagement rings—nice ones, all different sizes.

Drakon carried the case over to the study's window and held it out so it would catch the moonlight. I peered over his shoulder. It was amazing. The sparkling light and color that I could see from the diamonds with even the smallest amount of moonlight was spectacular.

Next, Drakon pulled out the stack of papers. "Oh my!" he exclaimed, "bearer bonds."

It had become apparent to both of us that Mr. McDouglas had an abundance of wealth, most likely that he'd gotten from illegal affairs. However, it didn't matter now. It was ours.

Thoughts were rushing through my mind. *I'm a millionaire. Oh yeah, Ferrari here I come. well, as soon as I get my driver's license. Let's see. What else?*

Drakon quickly interrupted my pleasant and somewhat ridiculous thoughts. "Sit down!" he said, pointing at a chair in the study. I sensed he wasn't really angry with me but more concerned.

He told me about his wealth. "After five hundred years, Michael, you must know that I have a lot of money saved up." He went on to explain that he had once lived a wealthy lifestyle, but he found it miserable. "It caused more problems than it helped—and it definitely doesn't bring you happiness."

"Hmm, really?" I questioned. Drakon just glared at me.

He went on to explain that he found living a middle-class life was the most fulfilling. "I know it's not the same, because I don't ever have to worry about money, but living a humbler lifestyle has made me much happier," Drakon said as he paused as if to see that I was getting it. He went on. "Besides, Michael, if you all of a sudden show up with a Ferrari, how in the world would you explain that to everyone? You know everyone would surely ask."

I was beginning to understand. I knew I couldn't just all of a sudden be some rich kid, *but what the heck do I do with all this money? And what's the point of having it all anyway?*

"Oh, we will split Mr. McDouglas' stash, of course," I said, feeling a little guilty that I'd almost forgotten about sharing it with Drakon.

Drakon laughed. "I don't need it, but thanks. This will be a good start for you. However, you will need to meet my banker friend to help you out with all this. On Monday, we shall visit Mr. Bill Green at the downtown bank."

We found some empty suitcases in a bedroom closet and filled both of them almost completely full. The one with the bullion was heavy, even for my brutish strength. "What do I do with this gold and silver stuff?" I asked as we were departing the neighborhood.

Drakon chuckled. "Well, that we can put into a safety deposit box for now. It will be like a rainy-day fund. I think there is enough other money that you shouldn't be needing to cash any bullion out right now."

I nodded. "Yeah, I guess."

"You guess. Really?"

I laughed. "Well, you know, Ferrari cars can cost a lot of money."

Drakon gave me a nice harsh shove down the alleyway.

Chapter Twenty-One

The Banker

We had to wait until Monday to go to the bank. Drakon would hold on to the goods until then. He told me to bring the briefcase that I had already confiscated along with me. I was to meet him downtown after school.

I found it hard to concentrate during my classes all day. What kid could? I mean, I was about to become a millionaire...but I had to hide it. *That sucks!* However, I dreamed of things I could get for Hadley. *But I have to hide the fact that it will be from me. She must never know. That sucks too.* I wondered how this whole money thing was going to work.

Three p.m. rolled around. I waited for Drakon in front of the downtown bank. About fifteen minutes went by. Finally, he came strolling down the sidewalk. "Michael, been waiting long?"

I scoffed. I looked down at my cell phone to check the time.

"Oh, come on." Drakon smiled as he opened the bank's front door.

We didn't head to a teller. We walked directly over to a side office. The door was already open. The plaque on the side of the door read *Bill Green, Marketing Representative*.

Before Drakon could even knock, a voice said, "Come on in."

A tall, thin man with thick-lensed glasses and a partially bald head stood up from behind a desk and shook Drakon's hand. "Long time, buddy. How is everything?"

Drakon and the man exchanged greetings and talked cordially for a few minutes.

"Well, what brings you in today, Drakon?" Mr. Green asked as he glanced over to me. I could tell he was curious about who I was and why I was there.

"I have another client for you, Bill — a special client, if you get my drift."

"Oh, I see. A client like us?"

"Indeed…and only sixteen at the moment. I believe he will need a special business set up to manage his funds."

The banker and Drakon worked for a long time sorting out some financial issues. The banker did a bunch of stuff on the computer and brought out all kinds of paperwork from his files.

The two of them finally decided to set me up with an LLC. Drakon would have to be the guardian over it until I turned eighteen. Also, the company name would not show my name. Someone would really have to look into it to figure out who the owners were.

Another issue came up. I had to use my legal name. This puzzled Mr. Green. It took him a moment to get it. "Ohh," he simply said, likely not knowing what else to say. It was almost embarrassing, but flattering that the man did not know any different. I had to sign every paper *Jenna Michelle Holliday.*

Drakon knew what I was feeling. "We should work on legally changing your name, don't ya think?"

I nodded and grumbled, "Definitely."

The other part of my finances had to do with the Caymans. Drakon told me these would be my offshore accounts. These were evidently nontaxable and untraceable. I could hide most of my wealth in these accounts.

Finally, Drakon placed a duffel bag on top of Mr. Green's desk. "The last of it."

Mr. Green unzipped the bag and peered inside. "Holy crap!" He rifled through the bag a bit more. He pulled out the small stack of papers, the bearer bonds. "Geez, Drakon, these are worth more than all of the cash you said you had. You know that, right?"

Drakon smiled and gave a slight nod.

"The bullion and the diamonds will need a safety deposit box, I presume?"

"Yes," Drakon answered, "for now."

The bearer bonds were worth one million dollars each. *Oh, man, am I rich – or my LLC is worth a lot anyway.*

Drakon and Mr. Green both gave me another lecture on using this money wisely. *What? Do they think I'm like a stupid teenager or something? Oh, well, yeah, I guess so.* Mr. Green told me that any time I needed a withdrawal, I had to come to him. It had to be a secret thing that I was the owner of the LLC, because I was still under eighteen and we didn't want anyone knowing about it, either. By no means was I to go on any spending sprees. *Geez, what is the point of having all this money?*

Drakon heard my thought. "Financial security, Michael, in your life – and to help others. You said you wanted to help Hadley. Why don't we work on that?"

That was exactly what we did. Mr. Green devised a plan. He would have my LLC buy a house. Then the LLC would offer up a fake contest letter to Mr. Johnson, Hadley's dad. It would represent a Housing and Urban Development program, also known as a HUD program for lower income families in which Mr. Johnson had won two years free rent. The issue was that Mr. Johnson was dead. How would we get Hadley into the house without officials finding out?

We finally decided that I would have to make Hadley believe it was a contest that her father must have entered before he died. After the two years' free rent, I would have to figure something else out. Maybe by then I could just tell Hadley the truth.

In the meantime, Hadley would get the letter in the mail. All that would be required to make it seem official would be Mr. Johnson's signature, which was where I would come in. I would have to persuade Hadley to falsify the signature. Drakon, Mr. Green and I would be the only ones to know. *This can work...hopefully.*

When all business was completed. I thanked Mr. Green and Drakon. Mr. Green would make up the fake letter and get it mailed off. Drakon would also get me set up with a post office box. That way all my business mail would go there and not be traced to my house.

Everything was done. My F2M bottom-half surgery? Well, it would still have to wait. I had too much going on right now.

Chapter Twenty-Two

A White Picket Fence

Life went on. I had replenished my thirst with Mr. McDouglas, therefore I hadn't felt any further lust for blood. School was going well. Callie, Junie and Jonathan were constantly bugging me about my powers, but otherwise things were pretty normal.

Hadley had found new happiness with not having to worry about rent for a few months and having enough money to cover food for her and Lily for a while. She and I were becoming better friends as each day passed. I managed to stop by her place after my gym workouts almost every day. I was also secretly snooping through Hadley's mail if I got the chance. I anxiously awaited the day for my LLC free rent giveaway letter to arrive.

Two weeks went by. I was beginning to wonder if Mr. Green had mailed the letter. Then the day arrived. I walked up the steps to Hadley's and I heard screaming from inside. First, I thought something was wrong, but I quickly sensed that these were screams of joy.

Little Lily had the highest pitched scream around. Most of the time I would cower from the sound, but today it sounded glorious. I knew what it meant — at least I hoped it was the letter.

Even through the shrieks and screams, Lily still must have heard the creak from the front steps because the door was flung open.

"Michael!" Lily grabbed my hand and pulled me into the house. "Guess what? Guess what?"

Hadley was leaning over the kitchen table, staring at a letter. I played dumb. "What, Lily? What?"

"Come here. Come look." Lily dragged me over to the table.

Hadley didn't say a word. She barely glanced at me, then with two fingers she pushed the letter across the table to where I stood.

I picked the letter up and pretended to read it. I already knew what it said. Right away I spotted the letterhead saying *Ns4a2*, my new LLC.

"Wow?" I replied, acting as though I knew nothing, "What's this mean?"

"I think Dad won a contest. He must have put in, um, well, you know, before he left," Hadley said, shifting her look to Lily.

Lily just rolled her eyes.

"Win what?" I asked, still playing like I was unaware.

"He won like free rent or something, I think. But look here… It needs his signature. What do we do about that?" Hadley asked as she tapped on a line at the bottom of the letter.

I almost laughed, just barely managing to contain myself. "I think we can manage to forge his signature, don't ya think? Do you have anything old of his with his signature on it?" I asked, although I knew it didn't matter, because I would be the one approving the letter. I was just playing along.

Hadley searched through some old paperwork in a kitchen drawer. She finally pulled out an old letter. "Here! Here's one!"

Hadley practiced writing her dad's signature for half an hour at least. Lily kept saying "You guys are going to get into trouble." We had to explain to Lily that this had to be a secret and that they could get a new house for free if they sent in the letter.

It was hard to get a five-year-old to understand sometimes, so I just promised her free ice cream once a week as long as she kept the secret.

"Michael!" Hadley complained.

"Whatever it takes." I was willing to use the needed tactics to make Lily keep the secret. Whatever worked.

It only took two days before my PO box got the letter. I took it straight away to Mr. Green so that he could get started on getting Hadley set up with the new house. He told me he would go by Hadley's as the representative of the LLC and set up the completion of the deal for as early as this next Saturday. He would meet Hadley at the new house with the keys. That way, hopefully, Hadley would invite me to come along.

The day after Hadley met with Mr. Green, she did exactly that. She invited me along. She didn't even wait for school to start. She was waiting for me on the sidewalk out front of my house that morning. Hadley was more excited than I had ever seen her about anything.

I laughed at her as I walked out of the door of the house. "You could have knocked and come inside. Where's Lily?"

"Oh, I dropped her off at her school already. I couldn't wait to tell you," Hadley said as she pulled the new house keys out of her pocket and dangled them in front of me.

"Oh, what's this?" I asked as I quickly snatched the keys from her hand.

She fought hard to get them back. I just held my hand out of her reach and laughed. "A new house?"

"Yes!"

I finally held the keys closer. She quickly grabbed them back. "Arggh!"

"Well, when? Do I get to see it?" I hinted.

"Well, if you would have given me a chance, I would have asked you."

I smirked.

"Saturday morning. You will come with us, right?"

I raised my eyebrows, paused like I was maybe thinking about if I wanted to go or not. "Of course. I want to check out this new house of yours." Really, I wanted to check out the new house that my LLC owned. I hadn't even seen it yet. I had just trusted Mr. Green to do the right thing. I hoped it was a good house.

Hadley slugged me in the shoulder for the delayed reply. We then talked about house stuff all the way to school. What might Hadley's new house be like? I told her it was only a HUD home, so it was probably nothing extravagant. I didn't want her to get her hopes up too high. However, she didn't care.

"It'll be better than a shack with an atrocious leaky roof — you know, one that leaks waterfalls."

I chuckled and nodded. "For sure — and maybe you'll have a bedroom to yourself."

For the rest of the week, Hadley talked about nothing but the new house. Even Junie, Jonathan and Callie were excited about the news. They were secretly working on a house-warming gift for Hadley. They wouldn't even let me in on the deal because they told me that I would probably spill the beans — and I'm sure they were right. That reminded me, though, that I needed to get a housewarming gift for Hadley.

* * * *

I was playing with my mashed potatoes Thursday night at supper. I still had no idea for a gift.

"What's on your mind, Michael?" Mom asked in her sweet tone.

I looked up from my mashed potatoes that I had so creatively piled up on my plate, and found both Mom and Dad staring at me. I grinned.

"What's up?" Dad asked with a raised eyebrow.

"Well…" I went on to tell Mom and Dad the Hadley story. I told them everything, except for the part of me being a vampire and the part where I'd killed her dad and her landlord, was a millionaire and had bought her a house. I told them that her dad was missing, maybe dead. I filled them in on her entire situation with Lily and all.

"Um, I sold my saxophone."

"What!" Dad exclaimed.

"Hush, John," Mom replied then softly said, "Go on, Michael."

I went on to tell them all about the saxophone sale and the money that I'd got from it. "But I spent half the money already. I paid for Hadley and Lily's rent for two months and gave them some money for food. Um, but they don't know it was from me."

Mom and Dad were silent. Mom's eyes got all watery.

"I'm sorry, Mom. I didn't mean to sell my sax and not tell you guys."

"No, no, sweetie, that's not it." She wiped a tear from her cheek as it rolled down her face. She smiled at me. "I'm so proud of you. I can't think of anything better that you could have done for little Miss Hadley."

Dad was just smirking, not saying a word.

"Really! Geez, thanks, Mom. Um, something else." I explained about Hadley winning a new rental house for two years. "I want to buy her a housewarming gift, but I don't have a clue what to get, and she moves in on Saturday. I'm in like panic mode. A little help would be great. Um, I still have like nine hundred bucks left from the saxophone sale."

Dad's eyes lit up. He chuckled. "Dang, didn't you buy that thing for twenty-five dollars?"

I laughed. "Yep."

Mom had some great ideas right away. "You should buy her stuff for the kitchen, a TV, bedroom sheets or throw pillows for the living room. She is going to need all of those kinds of things."

Shit! Bedroom, living room! I knew the house came with a fully furnished kitchen, but I had forgotten about the rest of the house. *Crap!* Lily and Hadley didn't have much in the way of belongings. *Oh, man, I need to call Mr. Green and fix this. What's a nice new house if you have no furniture for it?*

"Yeah, kitchen stuff. I think that's what I'll get. Thanks, Mom. Hadley's stuff sucks. I'll go tomorrow after school if that's okay." I was really thinking about the phone call I needed to make to Mr. Green.

"Yes, that will be fine. Want me to go with you and help?"

"Um, no thanks. I want to do this myself. You know, my gift." I didn't want to seem rude to Mom, but I really had LLC business to take care of too. She couldn't find out about that.

"Okay, dear, whatever you think. Call me if you need help."

I smiled at Mom and, on that note, finished my beautifully stacked mashed potatoes.

I didn't sleep well with the furniture dilemma on my mind. *Call Mr. Green. It will be okay.* I tried to tell myself that over and over and over.

* * * *

By my second class on Friday morning, I was going nuts. I finally asked Mr. Harsh if I could go to the restroom. He knew it would take me a while because he was aware that I always used the unisex bathroom in the new wing and that it was on the far side of the school building.

My real plan was to call Mr. Green. With a hall pass in hand, I quickly stopped by my locker and grabbed my cell phone. I started dialing as I made my way to the bathroom. I figured it was a good time to go to the bathroom anyway. That way it wouldn't really be a lie.

"Hello."

"Hello, Mr. Green, this is Michael. I have a big problem." I got right to the point and went on to explain that we forgot to furnish the house. I think my voice showed the panic I was feeling.

I heard a soft chuckle at the other end of the phone. "Michael, it's okay. I have an easy fix for that." He paused. I was impatient.

"What? What!"

"Stop by after school. I will give you a gift card that will be from the LLC. It will be for the local discount furniture store. You can tell Hadley that I contacted you and that it was a surprise or something. I don't know, just make something up like you kids do. See? Easy. Then you guys go and pick out what she needs."

"Phew. Okay. Yeah, I can make that work. Thanks, Mr. Green."

"Oh, no problem, Michael. That is what your company pays me for." He laughed.

Hmm, I wonder just how much I pay him. Drakon and I didn't ever really discuss the details. *Oh well, as long as he takes care of me and my LLC and Drakon trusts him, so I should too, I guess.*

* * * *

Saturday morning couldn't have come soon enough. I think I was at Hadley's door an hour early.

"Dang, Michael, you're here a bit early," Hadley said as Lily escorted me in through the front door of the shack.

I grinned. "Don't want to be late today." I held out both of my wrapped gifts. I sat the gifts down on the kitchen table.

"What's this?" Lily asked right away. "One for me? One for Hadley?"

I smiled. "Sorry, kiddo. These are for the new house."

"Ahh," Lily moaned, but then of course she started to unwrap the gifts.

"Lily! Not yet. We'll take them with us to the new house. Thanks, Michael."

I smiled then grabbed up the gifts again. Lily was still pawing at them. I chuckled as I gently had to keep nudging her away. She did make it difficult to keep the gifts tucked under my arms, the little devil.

We were early to the new address, 922 Morrison Avenue. It was not a wealthy area of town, but it was a nice, quaint neighborhood. It was just a middle-class kind of place.

I suspected Hadley had already been by the place several times, if only out of curiosity. I would have. It was a cute little house. It had a brownish-red brick exterior, like most of the homes in the neighborhood. It had a small front yard, which needed a bit of care. There was a white picket fence around the entire front yard, just like in a fairy tale, but like the yard, it also needed some work, some painting perhaps.

The house was narrow but had two stories. There was a driveway leading down the side to a carport that led to a door into the house. I assumed it was the kitchen door, kind of like mine.

Lily was trying to open the front door before Hadley and I had even entered the gate. We just laughed at her.

"Lily, I'm sure it's locked. We have to wait for the man from the bank or the HUD guy. He's bringing the keys to unlock the realtor's lock," Hadley said, shaking her head at Lily. Hadley already had keys to the house, but evidently a security lock had to be unlocked before it officially became hers. That was why we had to wait.

"Mr. Green," I added.

Hadley gave me a puzzled look. "How do you know?"

Oops, slip-up.

"Um, I know the man. I actually have an account at the downtown bank. Mr. Green knows me." I quickly muddled through an excuse.

"Hmm," Hadley mumbled as she gave me a little frown.

Mr. Green arrived moments later. I guess he knew we would be anxious and that we would most likely be there early.

He walked up to Hadley, Lily and me as we sat on the front steps. "So, where is Mr. Johnson?"

What? He knows what the story is. Why is he asking that? I raised my eyebrow at him. He gave me a little smile. *I guess maybe an adult would have to ask that. Otherwise, it would be kind of suspicious, wouldn't it?*

I looked over to Hadley. She looked panicked, so I spoke out. "Um, Mr. Johnson is out of town on a job."

"Oh, I see. No worries. I have all the properly signed documents already. I suppose I can hand the house over to Mr. Johnson's daughter."

Hadley gave me a look. I knew she was thinking about her forged signature. I just smiled and nodded for her to agree.

Mr. Green took off the security lock then said, "Oh yeah, the utilities are all included, thanks to the gracious LLC that supplied all of this."

I perked up. I hadn't even thought about that kind of stuff.

"Oh, and the Boys and Girls Charity threw in a two-year subscription for free Wi-Fi service. They thought it would be an aid in your education. Ahem." Mr. Green cleared his throat with the last statement and gave us all a serious look.

Yeah right, that's what us kids use the Internet for, education. Ha, okay, maybe a little research here and there.

Mr. Green excused himself, leaving us to explore the new home. Hadley took forever opening the door. I think she was almost afraid to open it.

"Come on, already. There's nothing in there to be afraid of."

Hadley gave me the stink eye. I chuckled as I took the keys from her trembling hand and unlocked the front door. Lily squeezed in before I could even get it open all the way. I calmly walked in and set my gifts down on the nice granite kitchen countertop.

The living room and kitchen were all one open space. I thought that was nice. It made the little house feel bigger somehow.

Lily was off like a jack rabbit. I think she had seen all the downstairs already and was headed up the stairs before Hadley had even said a word.

Hadley still stood in the entryway, silently looking around. Tears were rolling down her face.

"What?" I asked.

"I can't believe we were so lucky to get a new house."

I shook my head a little and chuckled. I wiped her tears from her face. *Here I thought she was crying because there was no furniture, but no, she doesn't even care about such small matters.* I found Hadley amazing.

"You deserve all this. It's about time something good comes to you and Lily. Oh, there's one more thing." I pulled out the furniture store gift card from my pocket. "Mr. Green gave me this. It was an extra surprise."

Hadley burst into a fierce bout of crying, like I had never seen, but I could tell it was a happy cry. However, I didn't know what to do. I was going to hug her, but that didn't feel like it would have been the right thing, so I just held her hand. Luckily, Lily came running up to the wooden railing at the top of the stairway.

"Guys, this is so awesome! I get the biggest bedroom. It has its own bathroom."

Hadley stopped crying and looked up at Lily. "Oh, I think not!"

I laughed. *Sisterly bickering, what a life saver.*

Hadley and I ran up the stairs, racing each other to the top. I won. Now that we were both in a glorious mood, we explored the second floor, talking and laughing. Of course, Hadley would get the big bedroom, but it took some convincing to get Lily to agree. We had to bribe her by telling her she could pick out her own bedroom set, which was what our next discussion was about—the gift card. What could Hadley possibly manage to get from the discount furniture store? How could she furnish the entire house?

"Don't worry, Hadley. This is plenty of money. I bet we can get furniture for every room, especially at the discount store prices. Plus, their stuff is pretty nice too. Oh yeah, my gifts… You haven't opened them yet."

Hadley laughed. "Better than a five-thousand-dollar gift card?"

I gave her a shove. "Maybe," I said sarcastically.

Hadley was actually appreciative of my gifts. I knew she would be. I mean, her dishes at the shanty were horrifying, so a new dish set was an easy pick for one gift. I'd also added a new silverware set, since I'd noticed before that she and Lily had often used plastic ones. The crockpot was an added bonus. I figured it made for easy cooking. Lastly for Lily, inside the crockpot I'd hidden a nightlight, a cool unicorn one. That particular model was very hard to come by, at least that was what the lady at the store had told me. However, the girls hadn't found that gift yet.

"Where's something for me?" Lily asked right away, like any five-year-old would.

I laughed. "What? You think you need something too?"

Lily glared at me. "Well, yeah. I do need stuff. This is my new house too."

I gave her an eye roll, which caused Lily to beat on me a little. "Michael!"

"Oh, all right." I finally caved and dug out her gift from inside the crockpot.

"No way! This is just what I needed!" Lily practically screamed.

Of course, I was sure anything would have been just what she'd needed. She cracked me up, but I was glad that she was easy to please.

Dinngg! Donngg! The doorbell rang.

Hadley and I were both surprised. Who knew she lived here already? I gave her an 'I don't know' shrug. Hadley slowly opened the front door as I peeked out of one of the front windows.

It was everybody! My mom and dad, Jonathan and Junie, Callie and her parents, Drakon, his wife and a little toddler. *Dang, I didn't know Drakon had a kid.* Lastly, Mr. Green and a woman who I assumed was his wife. Everybody was carrying gifts and what looked to be like food dishes. *Very cool.* I hadn't even known about the surprise. *This was what the dirty dogs wouldn't tell me.*

The kitchen counter was full of gifts and food. Hadley was grinning ear to ear. I don't think I had ever seen her so happy. She went on to show everyone around the house. Mom, Dad and I stayed behind in the kitchen to help set up the food.

"Well, what did you get her?" Mom asked.

I showed Mom my gifts and told her of Lily's unicorn light, which Lily had already taken away somewhere.

Mom laughed. *What? I thought they were good gifts.*

Mom pulled something out of the box that Dad had carried in. It was a beautiful bouquet of flowers in a light clear blue vase engraved with butterflies, something Hadley would really like. "Wow, Mom, Hadley will really like that."

Mom shook her head, chuckled and handed me a little card that went with the flowers and a pen. "That's why these will be from you."

"Hmm?" I gave her a puzzled look.

Dad actually rolled his eyes. "He's hopeless, dear."

Then it clicked. "Ohh, I see." Mom was trying to get me to give Hadley something a little more special, something a little romantic. She always did know the perfect gift, even if it was a bit mushy.

"Oh, Mom," I mumbled as my face turned hot.

I signed the card, nothing cheesy, just *Good luck in your new home, Love Michael.*

I did say 'Love Michael'. Was that too much? Geez, that scared me a bit.

Mom, Dad and I set out all the food. Callie's parents had brought a great cake. We put it in the center of everything. I swear there was enough food for an army.

All in all, the party was awesome. Lily had so much cake and ice cream that I thought her energy would never run out. It was definitely a sugar high for her. Later, though, I found her crashed out on the living room floor, and not even our loud conversations caused her to wake up.

Everyone finally cleared out. Hadley wanted to stay in the new house overnight, but there was no furniture yet—no towels, no clothes. None of her and Lily's stuff had been moved over yet. We still needed to shop for furniture. I had to practically drag Hadley and Lily out of the house. I finally convinced them to sleep one more night in their little shanty. *Can't blame them, I wouldn't want to go back to that place either.*

* * * *

I made Jonathan, Junie and Callie all help out the next day. Luckily, it was Sunday and not much was going on. I had promised Hadley we would get her out and into the new house. We moved over all of her and Lily's belongings, which wasn't much. I found it quite sad. I thought there would be more, but after leaving all the cruddy worn-out furniture behind, they really didn't have much. They had a small amount of clothes, a few of Lily's toys and a couple of odd items, which I thought should have been thrown away, but Hadley refused.

Having not taken long to move everything over to the new house, we all headed to the discount furniture store. The girls thought the furniture shopping was great fun. Jonathan and I were like 'enough already, just pick something'.

After what seemed like forever but was probably only a couple of hours, Hadley had picked out everything she needed for the house. She did so and managed to stay under the five thousand dollars that was allotted on the gift card. Lily even, like we promised, got to pick out her own bedroom set. I thought she was going to pick the hideous pink set, but, in the end, she picked an intricately decorated white one. It was actually very nice — a job well done by a five-year-old.

There was a one-week delivery date for the furniture, but Hadley didn't care. She wasn't going back to the shanty.

"We'll sleep on the floors for a week. No problem."

Jonathan ended up finding a couple of camping mats that he loaned Hadley for the week. Junie threw in a couple of pillows and blankets. So, all in all, they would survive.

Hadley and Lily didn't care. By the smiles on their faces, they were just glad to finally be in a place they would be happy to call home.

Chapter Twenty-Three

Impatiently Waiting

Hadley was unbearable to be around for the next week. At school, all she would talk about was her new house and when might the furniture arrive. Of course, I understood. This was probably the best thing that had ever come her way. It killed me, though, that this was all my doing and Hadley would not ever be the wiser. *How does it pay to be good if no one ever knows?*

The cool thing, though, was that Hadley had come out of her shell a little bit. She was talking more with all of us and even speaking up in class. Mrs. V, our English lit teacher, about fell out of her chair when Hadley answered a question one day. It was great to see Hadley so happy.

James and the boys tried to bother us at lunch that week. We were all in such a good mood that we didn't pay them any attention. I think that made them even more mad than if we had said something back, but we were having none of their shenanigans.

On Friday after school, we all headed over to Hadley's. It was the day the furniture was to arrive. We told her we would help her get everything arranged the way she wanted it, but mainly I think she just wanted us to see what the house would look like once it was furnished. She was so proud.

I had already told Mom about my plans and that I would probably be home late. She thought it was great and told me I could stay late if I wanted — but not too late. Mom did make me laugh.

Callie and I picked up some food from a local deli on the way over to Hadley's. I told Hadley we would meet her there and not to worry about snacks for all of us, that Callie and I would take care of it.

I knew Hadley was running short of money again. She hadn't been eating at lunch. I had to figure out a way to get her and Lily more money. *What story can I come up with this time?* I also knew Hadley had been applying for some after-school jobs. I'd seen an application for McDonald's in one of her school notebooks. I wondered, though, who would take care of Lily if she worked after school. I knew she was just trying to survive, but I didn't think that was an answer, not with Lily around. I had killed her dad. I needed to take care of them.

Jonathan, Junie, Callie and I all made it to Hadley's at the same time. There was no furniture yet, so, with all of us having the after-school need to feed going on, we decided to eat. We just sat around on the living room floor, like a picnic.

"We should just do this all the time," Lily said, making us all laugh because she was serious. "Who needs a table anyway?" she added.

"I don't know. She has a point. Look at us. We're doing just fine. Like Lily says, why do we need to use a table?" I asked.

"Oh, you two." Hadley rolled her eyes. She gave me a good shove, catching me off guard. My shoulders fell back to the floor, but I managed to keep my plate level. I didn't want to lose any of my food. I think Hadley thought I was trying not to make a mess on her new carpeted floor. I chuckled.

"It's here!" Lily exclaimed. *Dang, the girl has good hearing.* The furniture truck pulled up to the front curb. They didn't mess around. The two young men put each piece of furniture where Hadley instructed them to place it. They also put together the bed frames. After it was all said and done, Hadley didn't really need any of our help, but I think she was just glad we were there.

When the two men were done, they were stalling a bit, just standing around. One of them finally made an 'ahem' sound and gave me a look. I was clueless. A little mind reading was in order. *Are these kids going to tip us? What a bunch of idiots. I'm sure this will be a waste of a delivery.*

"Ohh," I mumbled. *We are dorks.* I dug into my pocket and nudged Callie and Jonathan. They gave me blank stares. *Yes, dorks.* I pulled out a ten-dollar bill. "Here ya go, guys. I know it's not much, but…well, here."

Then Jonathan caught on. He came up with a five and Callie followed up with some ones. *Well, that's better than nothing.* The furniture men graciously took the money and left. I heard one of them on the way out say, "Well, I thought we were going to get nothing there for a moment. I guess, since it was a bunch of kids, we best consider ourselves lucky to get what we did." They both laughed. *Whatever. They're just lucky we had any money at all. What kids usually have any extra money? Heck, I have loads, don't I?*

I must have had a big grin on my face because Callie asked, "Michael, what did you do?"

"Hmm? Me? Nothing." I chuckled.

Life was about as good as it got. I had everything going my way right now, money, good friends, a good home and a nice girlfriend. *I think she's my girlfriend.*

Everybody left after we got Hadley and Lily all situated. Beds were made, towels were set out in the bathroom, dishes were put away in the kitchen and one unicorn night-light was turned on in Lily's room. It was a regular little home.

I stayed around a bit longer and played Candy Land with Lily, then I took off to let the two of them settle on their own.

My walk home was peaceful. I dreamed of a day that I would have my own house and be the man of that house, a complete man. Maybe now that I had money, I could complete my lower-half transformation. I wouldn't have to burden Mom and Dad with finances. I just had to come up with a reason to explain why I had the extra money. I could say it came from a charity — an F2M charity, Changes Are Us. I laughed as I walked home. Maybe my LLC would start just that.

Chapter Twenty-Four

Flashing Lights

As I rounded the corner, a pulsating red light was illuminating the hedges along the sidewalk. It was rather mesmerizing. I was still daydreaming about things I could do with my LLC. I hadn't yet noticed what was down the street.

I peered down to the end of the block. Two houses in, at my house, was where the flashing red lights were coming from. An ambulance! *Is it really in front of my house? Is it there for someone in my house? Mom? Dad?*

I took off like a jaguar, the fastest I think I had ever run. I think I made it to the front yard in a matter of a few seconds.

"Michael!" Dad screamed in tears from the front yard. The back doors of the ambulance closed as I turned to see who it was, but I knew. I knew it was Mom.

"Dad! What? What happened? Is Mom okay?" I ranted.

Dad fell to his knees and put his face into his hands. It was bad.

I was confused. I didn't know what to do. I put my hand on Dad's shoulder and watched the ambulance drive down the road. The sirens and lights that I used to think were always so cool when I saw an ambulance or fire truck go by seemed to hold a foggy and eerie spell on me now. *Maybe this is a dream.*

Dad finally said something that stirred me from my spell. "Michael, we need to go to the hospital. I'm okay now. Come on. We need to go now!"

"Surely Mom will be okay," I said as I looked at Dad as we drove toward the hospital. I could see that he was trying hard to concentrate on driving, but he was struggling to keep it together. I put my hand gently on his hand that was atop the steering wheel. He took a deep breath then nodded.

I didn't even know what had happened yet, but I didn't want to stir up Dad's emotions any more, so I didn't ask. I tried instead to do a mind read.

Dad's mind was a mess. It almost hurt to try to read his thoughts. It made me almost break down. I had to cut it short. The most I got was that Dad thought Mom had had either a stroke or a heart attack, something big, something really bad. He thought she was dead!

Now I was freaked. *No, she can't be dead. She was fine when I left today.* I kept telling myself over and over. I denied myself that anything could be so wrong.

Then, I started to feel guilty. *I should have been home. I could have stopped this.* Then I had a brilliant thought. *I can save her, like Drakon saved me — but how?*

"Drakon! Drakon! Help! Help!"

Dad and I rushed into the hospital emergency room. Dad was frantically asking about Mom. A nice nurse escorted us to a private waiting room. She told us that the doctors were doing the best they could and that they would let us know something when there was news.

But how can I save her? Do I need to get to her and like…bite her? I don't know what to do.

Too much time had gone by—or so it seemed. I got up from the ever-so-uncomfortable waiting room chair. "Dad, I have to get something to drink. Want anything?" He shook his head.

I plodded out to the vending machine area. *"Michael,"* I heard in my mind. It was Drakon! I turned around to find him standing right behind me. He gave me a hug, like for the first time, but somehow I knew something was wrong.

"Can you help me with this?"

Drakon's face saddened. I could sense his answer before he said anything. "No, Michael. It's too late. She's gone already."

"What? No!" I screamed out. A few people around glanced over, but I didn't care at the moment.

I started to back away from Drakon. He reached out and grabbed my arm. He leaned over and whispered in my ear, "Michael, to have saved her, you would have to have been there at the exact moment that she passed. It is too late now. I'm sorry."

I pulled away. "Great, it's my fault."

Drakon was shaking his head. "No, Michael."

I ran out of the hospital, away from Drakon, away from Dad, away from Mom, my dead Mom.

Chapter Twenty-Five

The Burial, the Party, the Misdoing

It was the following Sunday. We were having Mom's burial and wake. We held the burial services all outside and kept it simple, like Mom would have wanted. She'd always said, '*I just want a Celebration of Life party whenever I die.*' So, rather than a normal wake, we would have just such a party.

I hadn't been to school all week. I hadn't talked with any of my friends. I had gotten a few text messages from Callie, but I'd ignored them all week long. Mainly, I had been hiding out in my bedroom. Dad would peek in once in a while to check in on me. He knew I just needed some time, as did he.

My thirst was starting to rise, but I was trying to ignore that too. I didn't know how long I could put it off. I was already mad enough, blaming myself for not being home in time to save Mom. If I had just come home earlier from Hadley's house...

Everybody was at the funeral—Hadley and Lily, Callie and her parents, Jonathan and Junie, their parents, Drakon and his family, the ladies from Mom's coffee group and lots of other adults I didn't know. Tears rolled down my face at the sight of all the people who had come to my mother's burial. I swear, I think Mom must have been liked by the whole town.

Mom was my rock, my go-to with whatever, whenever. *What am I going to do now? Damn, this sucks!*

A lot of people cried—heck, everybody cried. Dad bawled. Drakon calmed me through his thoughts. It helped. He reassured me that it wasn't my fault. *"Death is a part of life for many, just not for you anymore, Michael. You are going to have to learn to accept the pain of seeing others that you love in your life die. They will come and go, but each life that you know will be a beautiful thing. You should celebrate every good moment while you can."* His thoughts made me feel a little better, at least for now.

After the funeral, several of us headed to my house. It was time for the Celebration of Life party. Dad and Aunt Jeanine had put it together. My aunt had created a video that consisted of photos of Mom over the years. She'd put it to some of Mom's favorite music, mostly old Beatles songs. They had it playing on the living room TV in a loop.

Everyone brought food and drinks. It was definitely like a big party and should have been grand. However, everyone kept coming up to me saying, "Sorry for your loss" over and over. I was getting pissed.

I finally snapped. "This is supposed to be a celebration of Mom's life! It is supposed to be a joyful party, so quit making it so dreadful!" I belted out in the middle of the living room.

Everyone got silent. Hadley had been standing next to me for support. She whispered, "Michael."

"What!" I exclaimed as I shook my head in disgust then turned toward the door.

I heard Callie tell Hadley, "Let him go. He just needs some time."

I didn't need time. I needed some kind of vengeance. I also needed to replenish. I was angry at myself, at Dad, at Hadley, at Mom and, I don't know…at the world, I guess.

As I walked down the street, I tried to remember Drakon's advice, but it just wasn't helping right now. *I feel sorry for the first evil soul that crosses my path tonight.*

I was in such a rage that I almost didn't sense Hadley's presence. Evidently, when no one was paying attention, she'd snuck out to follow me. She was worried about me. She was quietly walking a block behind me, just keeping an eye on me. She had no idea what I was about to do but I didn't care.

I walked down the sidewalk that was across the street from the McDonald's. I was on my way to the sleazy part of downtown, looking for some lowlife scum-dogs. That was when I spotted James and the boys. They were hanging out by James' truck in the McDonald's parking lot.

At first, I was going to ignore them. *Just leave them be.* But no, James had to be an asshole.

"Hey, look, guys, it's the LBCAJT queer — or whatever they call themselves."

I stopped. "It's just Michael!" I hollered.

James and the boys roared with laughter. Little did they know that I was at the end of my rope.

"That's it," I mumbled as I crossed the street toward them.

"Ooh, watch out, guys, here he — she, whatever it is — comes. Oh, I'm soo scared." James laughed.

Yeah, ya better be.

Hadley was still watching from the shadows. She came closer, hiding behind a tree so that she could possibly hear and see what was going on. In my anger, I still only barely sensed her presence.

I was still dressed in my funeral suit. Naturally, James couldn't help himself. "Dressed like a man today. Hmm, but no girl on your arm. Couldn't get anyone to fall for you?"

I snapped. "No, you asshole. My mom's funeral was today!" I exclaimed as I charged James.

The other boys were caught off guard. I had James by his jacket collar before he or anybody else could even react. I threw him to the ground like a rag doll. The other boys stood there, their mouths dropped open, in shock.

My rage had taken over. I don't know if I totally vamped or not, but by the look on James' face and the fear in his eyes, I would say I did.

I had my hand on his chin. I was pushing it back to expose his neck. It was one of those foggy moments. I was in a full-on rage and lost in my dark self. Everything else had become only a blurry background. All I could see was the pulsating beat of James' carotid artery. I was ready to quench my thirst. I had forgotten that I had a whole crowd of boys watching.

Amid it all and just at the moment that I was ready to sink my teeth into James, I heard a faint cry, like something from a distance. "Michael! Don't!"

I paused, realized the sound was close and not so distant. I looked up, even though my eyes were blurred. I shook my head a bit to awaken myself from my darkened state and looked again. There in front of me stood Hadley with tears in her eyes. *Did she see me in my full monstrous state? What does that even look like?*

I looked back down at James. He had been screaming and apparently bawling. I imagined he'd feared for his life. I looked around. The other boys had fled the scene. I eased up my grip on James.

"Hadley," I said, my voice shaking.

She just stood there with streams of tears running down her face. I stood up. James quickly scurried away. I gave him no matter. It was Hadley who was important to me.

"Let me explain," I said as I held out my hands, like an expression of innocence.

She gave me a stare, a stare I would not forget, one of shame and guilt. She turned and ran down the street.

I knew what she had seen. She'd seen her father's killer.

Chapter Twenty-Six

Sloppiness and Good Friends Who Clean It Up

I stood there in the McDonald's parking lot for the longest time. I don't really know how much time had passed. I finally roused my thoughts enough to know that I still needed to replenish myself. Before I could fix anything, I had to take care of my thirst.

I turned right out of the parking lot to continue on my way to the bad part of town. I noticed James' group of boys parked down the street, watching me from a distance. I wondered what they had seen. *Would they dare follow me?*

I watched behind me as I ducked into an alleyway. No one was following me. The boys must have been scared. *What are they thinking? Will they spread rumors? Monstrous stories?*

I stopped. I concentrated. My mind shot through the streets until I fixated upon the group of boys.

"Did you see Michael? He was in a rage. He threw James around like a rag doll!"

"Yeah, man. I didn't know he was that strong. Dang, that was pretty savage."

"*Hey, guys, we should find James. We kind of left him there all alone. You know he is going to be mad at us.*"

"*You know what? Who cares? He's kind of a jerk to us, like all the time. Hey, maybe we should get to know Michael a little better.*"

"*Yeah, guys. He's like way stronger.*"

I laughed as I walked on. *What a brilliant group. I don't think they'll be a problem. Dang, what a group of traitors too. They just want to be with whomever they think is the strongest, leaving poor James out high and dry. Well, they're not going to be my friends.* I laughed some more.

I released my thoughts from the boys. They were a bunch of dorks. I moved my thoughts back to the task at hand—quenching my thirst.

Ducking in and out of the shadows of the dark alleyways, I finally made it to the rough part of lower downtown. It was quiet tonight, with only a few miscreants still lingering about. I stood in the shadows, just at the corner of an old brick building, and listened to their thoughts, searching for an evil-doer. Any would do tonight.

A rough-looking man stumbled out of a dive bar across the street. He was maybe a little drunk. I know Drakon had told me not to feast on anyone with alcohol in their blood, but I didn't care right at this moment. I concentrated on this man's thoughts, hoping he was a scum dog, a bad person. He was. He was thinking about stealing money from his ex-wife, knowing she would just be getting off from a waitressing shift. He would force her to give him her tip money that she had earned tonight. Evidently he did this often. He thought, *she owes me for all my misery.*

Yeah, I doubt that she caused his misery. He was a low-life of a man enough for me. He would be mine!

I followed the man into the small parking lot at the side of the bar. No one else was around. The man was fiddling with his car keys. I couldn't believe he was planning on driving. *He deserves to die.* I easily talked myself into this one.

As the man went between two vehicles, to what I figured was his car door, I attacked from behind. I was sloppy. I was mad and didn't care.

Whoa, definitely some alcohol in his blood. I didn't stop, though. I didn't know what it was like to drink alcohol. I had never tried it before, except maybe a taste of Dad's beer, but I found it disgusting.

I drank the man's blood, replenishing my needs. However, I didn't get the same revived feeling this time. The ground started to spin beneath my feet. My stomach churned and nausea set in. I started to laugh at the whole situation, not even knowing why I was laughing. It wasn't really funny.

"What the hell!" I mumbled after throwing up all over the dead body that now lay between the two cars in the parking lot. I stared at the man, then I simply stumbled away, weaving my way down the sidewalk, leaving my corpse behind.

I staggered all the way back to my side of town. The sidewalk was still spinning beneath my feet. My thoughts were a jumbled mess. I found myself in front of Hadley's new house. *I have to make her understand.*

There was still a light on. I tramped up to the front door and pounded on the door, too drunk to even realize that I could have rung the doorbell. With no patience, I pounded on the door again like an unrelenting savage. I really didn't know what I was doing. I was definitely drunk. Drakon had warned me. I hadn't heeded his lesson.

A side window opened. "What do you want, Michael? It's late! Go home! Just go home!"

"Come to the door so I can see you," I said as my words slurred.

"Argghh!" I heard a huge moan from inside.

After a few moments, Hadley opened the front door, but she didn't invite me in. I tried to step inside. I couldn't. *Shit! Is this one of those myth things? Drakon must have forgot to mention this one.* Obviously, I couldn't enter.

"You're not invited in," Hadley said in a very angry voice. "What the heck is wrong with you anyway? Are you drunk?"

I stood in the doorway like a fool. I didn't know what she had actually seen tonight at the fight. I didn't really know what to say, nor did I have any sense of what was going on at the moment. "What did you see tonight? You don't know everything," I blurted out stupidly.

"I saw enough — and I don't want to know any more. Go home, Michael."

I got pissed. "This is my house. You think somebody by a miracle just gives you free rent for two years and money like last time? Yeah, like that was all me." *Oh shit! What did I just do?*

Hadley stood there, silent. Then the door slammed in my face. *Crap!*

I pulled out the bracelet from my pocket. I had been waiting forever for a special moment. I had waited too long. I stared at it, the beautiful small bracelet, then let it fall from my grip. Tears rolled down my face. I turned from Hadley's now-closed front door and walked away.

Somehow, I made it home. I don't remember much, except for puking in the gutter along the way. I crawled up our front steps and lay on the porch, looking up into the night sky. I cried. I mourned for Mom and told her everything.

I must have passed out because I awoke the next morning in my own bed, still in my bloody clothes. Dad must have carried me upstairs. *Oh man, am I going to have some explaining to do.* It made me think about Dad, poor guy. I had been so selfish. I hadn't thought about his loss. He had lost the love of his life. I knew in that moment that I had to get my act together. Mom would want that.

I got up. *Oh, my head!* I threw my suit and shirt in the trash because they were so covered in blood that the shades of blue of my shirt couldn't even be seen any more. *Dang, more clothes gone to waste.* I laughed. At least my soul was starting to feel better, plus I knew I had plenty of money. *I can buy lots of blue shirts. Whoa, buddy, take heed. Listen to Drakon's lessons, you dummy. Spend my money wisely. Don't be a dork. Come on, Michael. Get your act together. Get Hadley back!*

After my shower, I headed downstairs. Dad wasn't up yet, so I cooked us both some bacon, eggs and toast. I even put on a pot of coffee and brought in Dad's paper. *Geez*, I was still nauseated. *Remember… Do not drink the blood of a drunk man!* Sweat rolled down my face. I moaned.

It was Monday morning. I hadn't been to school for a week. It was time I went back. *Oh crap! Did I leave a body last night?* I didn't exactly remember everything about the previous night, just blurry moments and images. I knew, though, that I had screwed it up with Hadley.

Dad finally came downstairs. He was dressed for work. I was ready to answer his questions about the bloody suit and shirt and passing out on the front porch—but he didn't ask. I guessed Dad surely knew that I was drunk and probably thought I had been bullied again. He probably thought that all the blood was because I had a bloody nose from being beat up, which in the old days used to be the case on many occasions. Maybe he didn't want to embarrass me. I don't know, but he just let it go, not saying a word about it. *Thank God — or maybe thank Mom.* She'd always known when to let things be. Maybe Dad had been paying attention after all.

Dad and I had a nice breakfast together—quiet, but nice. We gave each other an understanding smile when we parted ways.

* * * *

Callie, Jonathan and Junie were waiting for me at the front steps of the school building. It was good to see the smiling faces of my friends again. I also knew that they always forgave me, no matter how badly I may have been acting of late.

"Hey, look who the cat dragged in." Jonathan smarted off right away.

I pushed him backward off the concrete wall into the grassy hill. He just laughed. Callie and Junie went on to tell me about all the juicy gossip I had missed during the last week. It was all crap, but funny, and it took my mind off of things.

Callie saw Hadley sitting by the baseball field fence. She waved her over. Hadley just looked away.

Callie looked over to me and glared. "Michael, what did you do?"

"Ohh." I sighed. "That's a long story."

Callie gave me the evil eye. I did want to tell her, mainly because I wanted her help—just not right now. "Later," I said as, thankfully, the first bell rang. *Drrriiinnngg!*

As I was getting out my trig book, Noah, one of James' boys, stopped as he was walking by. "Hey, Michael, what's up?"

I turned. "Um, hey," I simply replied.

"Later," Noah said in a really polite voice as he walked off.

I shrugged. *Strange.* I kind of knew what was up. I figured James' squad was still thinking about defecting. They were going to try and befriend me now that they knew I was stronger than James. Well, I wouldn't have it. *I don't want those jerks around. They've never been nice to me or any of my friends. Duh, what do they think? That I'll just drop my friends and join up with the likes of them? I think not! Dorks!*

As I walked down the hall toward class, Drakon's voice entered my mind. *"Are you okay?"*

"Yeah, I think so. Thanks. Um, I'm not so sure about last night though. I should have listened to you. I didn't." I concentrated my thoughts back as I slowed my pace to stall my arrival to class.

"I know already, but I imagine that you have learned your lesson now — the hard way. Plus, I know you had a tough time with your Mom's death, so I'm going to let this one slide. Sometimes we make mistakes in life and get knocked down. We just have to get back up on our feet."

Dang, Drakon was good. *"Yeah, I guess. I'm sorry, man. Um, but I don't exactly remember. I think I may have left a mess last night."*

I heard Drakon chuckle in my mind. *"You did. A horrendous mess, but I had your back. I was watching you. I knew you were having a bad week. I took care of it. All cleaned up. No evidence left behind."*

"Oops. Sorry again."

Drakon laughed. *"Just get to class, and I hope today is better."*

I chuckled. *"It's got to be."*

I had been concentrating so hard on my mind conversation with Drakon that I wasn't paying attention to where I was going. Dang if I didn't run right into someone. I looked up. The dude towered a foot over me. "James! Of course, it's you," I said out loud.

James quickly cast his eyes down to the floor. He was cowering before me. "Sorry," he mumbled.

I raised my shoulders and looked at him with my eyebrows raised. He stepped aside and quickly scurried away like a scared mouse would run from a big old alley cat. I looked around to see if anybody might have noticed. There stood Noah and Ethan, two of James' boys. They were standing there, just watching. Both boys gave me a wave. I gave them a little salute-like wave and walked on. It was weird, but kind of neat, at least uplifting for my ego. *Am I the school's Alpha male now?*

I chuckled as I walked on to class — getting several strange looks along the way, but I didn't care. I finally realized that it didn't matter what they thought.

I did better in my classes. I was finally able to concentrate on schoolwork for a change. English lit came around. Hadley was sitting in her usual chair. I slid into the desk next to her. I got a stink eye, then she got up and moved. *Not good.*

Lunch came around. I looked for Hadley, but she didn't come into the lunchroom. *How can I get her back if she won't even talk to me?* I didn't really remember everything I had said or done on that horrible evening. *Was it that bad?*

At lunch, I told Callie, Jonathan and Junie all about what I had done — at least the parts I could remember. I also explained to them about the purchase of the house and my new LLC company. Oh man, did that open up a whole lot of questions. I told them that lunch wasn't long enough to go over it all and we could talk about it later. I knew they wouldn't let that one rest. I would try to draw their attention back to my problem with Hadley. "I don't know if Hadley saw me vamp. I think she knows that I killed her dad. I think maybe I told her that her new house was mine."

Callie and Junie were kind of mad at me, but Jonathan reminded them about my Mom's death. He whispered it, but I heard him. Anyway, in the end, like all good friends, they forgave me and decided that Callie and Junie would work together to convince Hadley that I meant well. They would persuade her that her dad's death had really been self-defense on my part, which was true.

My friends liked Hadley too and they wanted her back in the group, so the plotting began. Every chance Callie and Junie had all the next week, they worked on Hadley, explaining my situation — every part of it.

I was to stay out of it and just be patient. That was tough, but I listened to my friends. I wasn't going to screw it up.

Friday came around. I had behaved all week. The third period English lit bell rang. *Drrriiinnngg!* The sound of the bell made me nervous. *Have Callie and Junie made any headway?*

As I entered the classroom, I saw Hadley sitting in her usual spot, looking as cute as ever. I took a deep breath and slowly walked to the desk next to her, sat down and waited for her to give me the old stink eye and move. She didn't!

Hadley pushed up her sleeve a little. There it was, the bracelet that I had dropped, the bracelet that had always been meant for Hadley. I chuckled then just eased back into my chair.

"So, Ns4a2? Really? That's what you named your LLC, Michael?" Hadley shook her head, but she chuckled and gave me a little smile.

Yes, I have a chance!

Chapter Twenty-Seven

For Those Who Just Want a Little More

It ended up Hadley wasn't mad that I'd killed her father. She'd kind of suspected it and understood how he could be when he got really drunk. She was mad at me for keeping everything a secret. I had told my other friends everything, but not her.

"You're a vamp. Really? And you don't think you might want to tell me?" That was what she'd said to me when she'd complained about it. I told her everything, all of my secrets, even my transgender ones.

She laughed at me. "You don't think I didn't know that already? I've known you since elementary school."

She did explain that she had paid attention to me since we were kids and I had just noticed her this year. I didn't have an answer for that. She could hold that one over me forever.

Our relationship became even closer. She knew what it was to lose a parent. I was able to talk to her about losing my mom and she could relate. My other friends didn't quite get it.

I was spending a lot of time with Hadley. I knew Dad was lonely and having a rough go of it, so we tried to include him in things once in a while. Hadley, Lily and I would try to spend more time at my house. Dad loved that. He would cook us all dinner and we would spend time around the table chatting, like a nice little family.

I'd finally told Dad everything. I told him all about the Nosferatu stuff, the LLC and even the killings, explaining that I had tried really hard to search out only evil souls. It felt really good to let him in on my secrets. All my friends knew, so why not Dad? At first, he didn't want to believe it, but deep down he'd always known something was going on. He actually came around pretty easily. He especially liked the LLC idea, and when Drakon gave me some leeway, it allowed for Dad to get out of debt. All in all, Dad knowing my secret had made him happier. As for me, I was happier too.

It was good for Lily, anyway. I think Dad was a good influence on her. She got to see what a proper Dad was like. He even taught her how to ride a bicycle.

So life went on, and it was pretty damn good. I still had to take part in an evening feast once in a while, but I was getting better at it — and no more drunks. Drakon was still teaching me the ways of a Nosferatu life. My friends were helping me hone my skills. I think they enjoyed experimenting with them more than I did. All in all, I was evolving into a better vamp, a better man. Good friends turned out to be the greatest support in my life. They always seem to stand by me, no matter what issues I faced — and man, did I have issues.

Lastly, all I needed was the completion of my F2M transformation. I got Mr. Green to set up a charity through my LLC. It was set up for all LGBTQ children, teens or young adults in the region. A couple of moms and a local doctor who specialized in the field sat on the board. They were all great.

There was more interest in the area than I had expected. The charity raised extra money through donations and fundraisers. My own funds were hardly affected.

By the way, my funds were doing great. Mr. Green had me make some investments and the money seemed to be pouring in.

The charity board would set up the help needed for each case that came their way, whether it was medical needs or even psychological care, like therapy. The local interest in the charity grew phenomenally and many more parents with kids like me around the region became involved.

As for me, I got my F2M lower-half surgery process all set to go. It would be a long one, not easy and not pleasant, but I was most certainly ready for the change.

I changed my name in court. It hadn't really sunk in yet, but now I felt the change in my soul.

I am no longer Jenna Michelle Holliday. I am Michael Jay Holliday!

Want to see more like this?
Here's a taster for you to enjoy!

Sharing Secrets
Matthew J. Metzger

Excerpt

Adam's morning was routine. Breakfast—seven o'clock. Shower and get dressed—seven-thirty. Ignore Mum's warning about being late for school—anywhere between seven and eight.

Right before that last warning, at eight-thirty every morning, knock back a pill and stare into the bathroom mirror.

"Adam! Hurry up, you're going to be late!"

"Nobody knows," Adam whispered to his reflection, just like every other morning. School mornings or weekends, home or holidays—every morning Adam looked himself in the eye and said, "Nobody knows."

"Get a move on, love!"

Of course people did. Some people. But nobody outside the family. Nobody in this new life, new place, new school. *Especially* the new school.

"Coming!" he yelled and frowned at himself in the mirror again. "Nobody knows."

Nobody outside this family knew. Or ever would.

"Adam!"

He grabbed his bag from the landing and hurtled down the stairs at full pelt. His mother flung his blazer at him in the hall and shouted a goodbye before he slammed the door and sprinted down the front path to the only other person in the village who attended Sir Henry Grey's Academy.

"Hi, Adam."

"Hey, Phoebe," he said, unchaining his bike from the gate. "Sorry. Let's go."

Nobody knew.

Adam was the new kid. Sort of. Okay, he'd started in September and it was now April, but he was still the new kid. Sir Henry Grey's was in the middle of a lonely clutch of villages in Gloucestershire and people didn't really come and go very often. He'd be the new kid around here for the next decade or something.

It wasn't all bad, though. Country kids were generally nicer than city kids—and Adam had been shuttled through enough inner-city schools to know. Leaving Manchester had been the best thing ever. And okay, the village he lived in was about two hundred people strong and boring, but...the school was better. The kids were all right.

"Guess who's fucking *leeeeeegal!*"

...but kind of crazy.

Turning up to see a girl standing on a chair and bellowing at the top of her lungs had been normal in Manchester. It usually involved knives and the word "slag" a lot. Here it involved—

"Ollie! Happy birthday!" Phoebe shrieked, bouncing once on the balls of her feet before sprinting across the canteen toward her. Phoebe, like Adam, was very fair. Ollie wasn't, with dark eyes, dark curls and dark skin. The hug that Phoebe bestowed on the birthday girl looked…kind of like a squashed yin-yang symbol.

Or a squashed Liquorice Allsort.

"Look!" Ollie said when Adam got acceptably close enough. She climbed up onto the table and lifted her skirt right up to her waist. Half the canteen gawped. The other half were too used to her and kept chattering. "Check it out!" she crowed.

"Is that a *tattoo?*" Phoebe gasped. An ornate black symbol of a butterfly decorated Ollie's bare thigh. Adam wrinkled his nose. *Lady legs.*

"Gorgeous, in't it?" Ollie grinned. "Mum let me!"

"Oh, my God, is that *real?*"

"Nah, but it will be, only two more years!" Ollie beamed.

"Miss MacFarlane, get down!"

Ollie rolled her eyes and slid off the table as the chubby headmaster, Mr. Weeks, stalked through the canteen. Adam had seen more intimidating chickens, but then he was used to schools where the kids tried to stab one another—or him—rather than ones where a girl could stand on a table, flash her knickers and not get so much as a wolf whistle.

Or maybe that was Ollie. Nobody would dare wolf whistle Ollie.

"So!" Ollie thumped her folded arms on the table and grinned. She had an enormous smile with Hollywood teeth—perfect, pearly-white and kind of plastic. Ollie was all sports, wild ideas and parties. Phoebe was pale, delicate and refined. Adam hadn't yet worked out what they had in common, but apparently they were friends. "You guys are coming tonight, right?"

"*Duh!*" Phoebe said, beaming in turn. "It's your sweet sixteen—of course we're coming! And we got you the perfect present—*but!*" she added when Ollie's face lit up. "But you don't get it until tonight. It's not safe for school."

"Awesome," Ollie breathed, and turned those dark eyes on Adam. Her smile was wild and Adam squirmed under the scrutiny. "Did you have a hand in this, new kid?"

Adam flushed as Phoebe smirked. "Oh, he chose it," she said.

"Didn't."

"You so did," Phoebe insisted, shaking her head. Her fair hair slithered around her shoulders, already falling out of its messy ponytail.

"Hidden depths, you have," Ollie sniggered, then slid her gaze past Adam and shrieked, "Charlie! Charlie, you *dick*, where you been?"

Adam's heart stopped.

"Move it, you lazy twat—you're late!"

Adam's heart restarted as Ollie jumped up and pounced on the newcomer—a lanky kid in a crumpled school uniform who managed to look startled every time she hugged him, although Ollie spent more time hugging Charlie than not. But it wasn't the hug that threw Adam.

It was Charlie himself. The sight of him knocked the wind out right out of Adam and threw off his equilibrium, and just like every other time, Adam couldn't—

"Shut your face, and what's this about you getting your knickers out, you tart?"

—breathe.

Charlie Fielding was, in Adam's opinion, beautiful. He shouldn't have been—he was the exact opposite of Adam's type. He ought to have been uninteresting...only he wasn't. He was *gorgeous*. Who cared if it sounded girly? He *was*. And he wasn't at the same time, which only made him more beautiful — and shut up, it made sense. Charlie was…

Charlie was all lanky build and wide, thin mouth. He had dark hair that was never tidy or properly cut, caught somewhere between curly and wavy, and bright blue eyes that were the exact color of summer skies and mania. Yes, mania had a color and it was the color of Charlie Fielding's eyes, *so shut up already*. He had long limbs, long fingers, long feet and…he was just long in general. He was this huge smile and talking-with-his-hands and he'd sort of grin and duck his head when embarrassed in a way that made Adam's stomach twist, and…

And he was completely, totally, absolutely off-limits. Forever. There was no way it would, could or should ever happen.

But it didn't stop Adam's gut from clenching at the sight of him or his heart simmering in jealousy when Ollie had bounded across the linoleum and jumped on Charlie in a hug. Sometimes, Adam hated Ollie a little bit. She could touch Charlie. She could be all over him in public and in private. She didn't have to be afraid.

But then when she touched him, Charlie would laugh and that pale face would light up like the bonus round on a pinball machine, and Adam *loved* her for that look.

Phoebe nudged his foot under the table and Adam swallowed and looked down. It was hard to tear his gaze away from Charlie's magnetism and when it fell on Phoebe, she cocked her head. She was smiling and Adam shook his head.

"You should tell him," she whispered and he shook his head again. "You *should*. You could, you know —

he'll be there tonight, too, and you'll be able to separate him from Ollie long enough…"

He kicked her under the table and she rolled her eyes. Phoebe thought him shy. Adam was happy to let her think it — anything was better than the truth.

"Even if he doesn't —"

"Gossip!" Ollie cheered, pouncing on Adam from behind in a hug. "Even if who doesn't what?"

Adam shrugged her off awkwardly, flushing, and she wriggled in next to Phoebe to hug her instead. Ollie was incredibly huggy and Adam hadn't worked out yet whether she'd taught Charlie or Charlie had taught her.

Probably a bit of both, he decided, as Charlie crowded into Phoebe's other side and she got squashed between them, her blondeness framed by black.

"Nothing," he said.

"Lies!" Ollie said. "C'mon, it's my birthday, it's my sixteenth, you have to tell me."

"We were saying," Phoebe said and Adam's throat tightened in fear for a moment. "At this party — Charlie, you keep your hands out of those pockets," she interrupted herself to scold, and Charlie pouted at her in an exaggerated fashion.

"But I can feel lumpy things!"

"Chocolate, you perv, and it's mine," she said. Ollie cackled. "Anyway. We were saying that Nate in my drama group totally fancies you, Ollie, but if he's not brave enough, we'll lock you two in a cupboard together tonight."

"Ew!" Ollie shrieked. "Ew, no, no-no-no — my birthday, not allowed!"

Charlie's eyes gleamed and a wicked grin spread across that narrow face. Adam's heart rattled like an engine on the brink of stalling.

"Nate has a crush on you?"

Phoebe was released as Charlie launched at Ollie instead to begin a merciless campaign of teasing and she stood up and pulled on Adam's arm. "Come carry books for me," she said and Adam let himself be towed. Phoebe had practically adopted him when he'd arrived and even though he was almost a clear eight inches taller than her, he appreciated her easy acceptance and the free ticket into not being a sad loner and a prime target for other kids to pick on. So much so that he just let her drag him along. Anyway, Phoebe was nice. Proper nice, not evil-nice like Ollie.

"You know," she said, halfway to her locker, "you should tell him."

"Tell who what?"

"Tell Charlie," she said patiently, "that you like him."

She'd caught him out around Christmas. He'd been staring just a little too much. Adam was just quietly grateful Charlie hadn't noticed yet. Because the answer was—

"No."

"He won't freak out."

"He might," Adam said. He probably wouldn't, actually, Charlie was really relaxed about that sort of thing. He'd be dead nice about it, but it was out of the question, anyway.

"No, he wouldn't," Phoebe insisted. "Tell him tonight! Then if he turns you down, you've got all weekend to deal with it, right?"

Adam swallowed and curled his toes in his shoes at the fleeting fantasy that—in some other universe, where it would be okay—Charlie would actually kiss him at this party and he'd have all weekend to worry about whether it was too soon to text him.

Then he crushed the fantasy. Brutally, under the heel of his shoe. Until it squealed.

"I can't, Feebs," he said eventually, holding out his hands for her books as she unloaded her locker. "I just...I can't, okay?"

Her face softened and she squeezed his wrist. "You should," she insisted but then let it go and asked if they really should lock Ollie and Nerdy Nate in a cupboard together.

Adam voted yes and tried to forget about Charlie at a party without Ollie on his arm.

* * * *

Ollie's parents were cool.

Ollie bitched, but Mr. and Mrs. MacFarlane were the coolest parents ever. They'd gone off to visit Ollie's nana for the evening and left them the whole house for the party, under the 'supervision' of Ollie's older brother, Jamie.

And judging by the fact Ollie was always being supervised by Jamie and Adam had never even seen Jamie, he was beginning to suspect that Jamie wasn't actually real.

Still, the house bulging with people was a bit intimidating and Adam inched through the front door feeling a little tense and a lot nervous. He'd never been to a house party before and felt faintly surprised every time he bumped into someone and they didn't recoil. Felt calmer every time someone greeted him by name and not...not some jeer, some sneer, some slur.

Then he learned to breathe again when Phoebe materialized out of thin air and hugged him.

"There you are! Here," she added, pressing a bottle into his hand. An orange-flavored alcopop. "I snagged it for you before Ollie could break into the cabinet. She's got her dad's liquor out — he's gonna kill her."

Adam seriously doubted that. Mr. MacFarlane had books called Open Dialogue With Your Teenage Daughter and Expression and Creativity — Rebellion in Young Adults. He'd probably praise her lock-breaking skills or something.

"She hasn't got round to presents yet," Phoebe confided and Adam pulled a face.

"Good?"

"It was your idea!"

'It' was a — well, a dildo, actually, that they'd bought online last week using Adam's sister's credit card. Phoebe had even added some condoms to the box, with a note saying 'now you're legal and all.' Adam wished he'd never used Nat's Amazon account to do it — he'd learned way too much about his sister's browsing history.

"Wasn't," he said weakly and Phoebe giggled.

"Totally was," she said then stepped back and did a little twirl. "What do you think?"

She was...actually dressed up for once. Phoebe was very pretty but very natural — as far as Adam could tell, not being into girls. Lady legs and stuff. She always just threw on her uniform and wore her hair messy and haphazard and her socks never matched, but tonight —

"Are you wearing makeup?"

She blushed.

"You are."

It looked...good but kind of weird, too. Adam decided he preferred the freckles. But the weird basket-weaving thing she'd done with her hair was kind of nice. Kinda sci-fi with the sparkly silver dress, too.

"Josh Denbar's here," she whispered and blushed harder.

"Oh." Josh Denbar of the way-too-long fringe and old-enough-to-smoke gorgeousness. Apparently. Adam thought his eyes were too close together. And that he wore weird shoes.

"And he broke up with his girlfriend this morning. So." Phoebe spread her hands and smiled shyly. "What do you think?"

Adam blinked. "Um. You might want to ask a girl. Or a straight guy."

Phoebe laughed and hit him on the shoulder. "Look out," she confided. "Hannah Barfoot has her eye on you."

"Um, what?"

"Yeah. And—"

"Hey!"

Ollie's voice boomed over the chatter. She was standing on her mum's prized coffee table, thankfully not so alien as Phoebe—because if Ollie had voluntarily put on a skirt, Adam would have to go home and call a doctor or something because what the hell—and holding a couple of vodka bottles aloft.

"Let's play Seven Minutes in Heaven!"

Across the room, Adam locked eyes with Hannah Barfoot—a giggly ginger girl in their year who reminded Adam a little bit of an overexcited puppy.

"Oh, hell no," he whispered.

"Run!" Phoebe whispered in his ear and Adam ducked backward through the clusters of people. He didn't know much about house parties, but the movies always said the same thing, right? When in doubt, make for the kitchen.

He made for it—hard—and snapped the door shut on the cackles and cheers behind him. No Hannah Barfoots and cupboards. No anybody and cupboards.

He couldn't. He couldn't, he'd—he'd have to give himself away and—

"Hiding?"

Adam spun around and flushed hotly at the sight of Charlie sitting on the kitchen counter, hand in a packet of sweets. Starbursts. He had ripped jeans on and Adam could see one bare kneecap.

"Oh," Adam said. "Um. Sorry. I'll just…"

"Not a party fan?"

Adam's flush deepened. "No," he said flatly. "I didn't get invited to many back…at my old school."

Charlie 'aah'ed and rolled his eyes, sliding down from the counter as someone banged on the door. "C'mon," he said, seizing Adam's wrist in one of those long-fingered, bony hands. Strange hands. "Ollie's dad has this cool shed. Let's hide there."

Adam let himself be towed into the darkness of the back garden—because anything was better than Seven Minutes in Hell with Hannah Barfoot—and soon they were swallowed by the night and the only thing he knew was the iron grip of Charlie's thin fingers around his arm.

"In here," Charlie whispered and Adam's trainers went from the soft squish of damp ground to hard wooden boards, and a door closed.

"It's dark," he complained.

"Hang on—ow! Motherfucker!"

Adam sniggered then a light came on—a lamp, in fact, on an upturned bucket. The shed was full of odd bits and bobs and Charlie shoved what looked like an old chest of drawers sawn in half in front of the door.

"There," he said. "Nobody'll see the light. Pull up a bucket and get comfy. They'll have all forgotten about us in half an hour and we can sneak back in."

"Ollie throws a lot of parties?" Adam guessed.

"Nah, not Ollie, but Megan — you know, ginger Megan in Mrs. Thompson's group — she does. Ever fancy a snog, get on her — she's right easy."

Adam grimaced. "Not…really my type."

"What, easy girls aren't your type?"

"No," he said and Charlie laughed.

"Good on you, mate," he said and raised his hand. "Five me."

Adam clapped his hand and curled his toes in his shoes at even the brief contact. Dear God, he was fucked. He was that hopeless to find a high-five amazing and he was shut in a shed — alone — with the giver of the five.

"Starburst?" Charlie asked, offering the packet. Adam picked out an orange one. "So what's your type, if not ginger Megan?"

Adam shrugged. "Um. Dunno really. Nice…girls. Nice girls. You know. With, um. Personality."

"Like Feebles?" Charlie asked.

"Well…not Phoebe, no, but…like Phoebe, I guess."

"Don't blame you," Charlie said, unwrapping a Starburst. His hands were oversized, the knuckles huge, and his fingers twitched and shivered as he worked. Adam stared, fascinated. He had never had the nerve to properly look before, but — Charlie's hands weren't just weird, they were actually deformed. "She's sweet, Phoebe. Knows how to keep a secret, too. She's not totally gossipy like Ollie."

Adam laughed. "Thought you and Ollie were joined at the hip?"

"Yeah, means I know how gossipy she is!"

Adam relaxed and perched on a wooden box. "What about you? What kind of girls do you like? Apart from Ollie."

"I don't fancy Ollie."

Oh. "No?"

"Nah, she's like my sister. That'd be weird. I've known her since we were like…four? Five? Little, anyway," Charlie said. "Actually, she's not my type, either, so even if I'd met her yesterday, I wouldn't fancy her."

"What's your type, then?" Adam pressed. He felt kind of safe, a little bit. He usually dreaded having to talk about girls, but Charlie was just…funny and casual and gorgeous and he seemed so — so not-probing-even-though-he-was-asking-questions that Adam just eased into it and lied and…didn't feel bad about it.

Because, really, in a shed on their own was a bad time, Adam figured, to tell his straight crush he was exactly Adam's type.

Charlie pulled a face. "You don't get a lot of time to meet girls with Ollie scaring off the competition. I mean, don't get me wrong, she's 'mazing and I love her to bits, but she'd scare the shit out of them Islamic State bomber nutters, man."

Adam laughed. "Yeah, maybe."

"So where'd you move from?"

"Um."

Charlie squinted at him in the low light of the lamp. "You know, I don't know nothing about you."

"Anything."

Charlie snorted. "Feebles, like, adopted you, but I don't think you and me ever had a conversation." They hadn't. "Or been alone together." They hadn't. "Fact, this might be the first time I've heard you say more than like ten words." It probably was. "So c'mon, new kid, where you from?"

Adam drew his foot away from the prod. "Manchester," he said. "Mum got a new job so we moved."

"What's she do?"

"Lawyer."

"Ew," Charlie said, wrinkling his nose. He had a long, straight nose, but it crumpled in the middle when he did that and creased up all his freckles. It was weirdly…kissable. Adam bit his lip. "My mum's a farmer. Stoker Farm. My granddad left it to her because my uncles are wasters. His words," Charlie added with one of those huge, manic grins. "Granddad was awesome. He used to take me shooting up in the top field because he said I was the only one in the family who could hit a barn door from ten feet away so I might as well have it."

Charlie's wide mouth and huge eyes were excitable and crazy and Adam just laughed. "Really?"

"Yup!"

"That's brilliant. You gonna be a farmer, then?"

"Naaaah," Charlie drawled. "S'boring. Dunno what I'm gonna do yet, though, m'no good at English and stuff."

Adam privately thought he had to be good at something. Farmers were usually poor, right? And Sir Henry Grey's was a private school. Charlie had to have gotten in there somehow.

Then Adam realized he was leaning too close and staring.

Shit.

"Reckon we can go back inside?"

"Probably," Charlie said, jumping up off the sawn-off chest of drawers and hefting it aside to peer out of the door. "Yeah, maybe. You wanna risk it? Hannah might catch you again. She right fancies you."

Adam flushed. "No, she doesn't."

"She does." Charlie grinned. "She's been making eyes at you since you got here, Ads. You're her type, even if she's not yours."

"You never said your type," Adam said, trying to distract him. He didn't want to get set up or anything. And girls didn't usually like him anyway, so Charlie was obviously wrong.

"Mine?" Charlie's eyes were glittering and almost white in the light of the lamp. "Me, I prefer blonds. No 'e.' If you know what I mean."

"No 'e'?" Adam echoed, bemused, then —

Then Charlie leaned forward and kissed him. There were...there were lips on his, lips that tasted like lime Starbursts and felt chapped and rough and vaguely sticky from the sweets. A mouth a little wide and a lot warm and Adam's heart was trying to punch its way out of his ribs. Charlie was kissing him. Charlie Fielding, the gorgeous and funny and brilliant and amazing Charlie bloody Fielding — was kissing him. His...those hands, those weird pale hands were on Adam's sides and he was tilting his head and Adam could feel his tongue, and —

And Adam could feel his tongue.

Adam was being kissed.

Instinct kicked in and he planted both palms on Charlie's chest and shoved. Hard.

"Fuck!" Charlie yelped, tumbling into the mess inside the shed, and startled blue eyes stared up at Adam. Adam felt panic rising in his chest like a tsunami and put both hands over his mouth to stop himself blurting something out. "What the hell, Adam?" Charlie demanded. "I just —"

Adam bolted.

Sign up for our newsletter and find out about all our romance book releases, eBook sales and promotions, sneak peeks and FREE romance books!

About the Author

Laurie is a retired fire captain. She lives in the desert of Nevada in the winter and roams the mountains of Colorado in the summer. After a bicycle accident and a bad brain injury, Laurie, who was once more of a math/science kind of gal, now finds the creative part of her brain kicking in. She has been writing ever since. Any local coffee shop makes for a good place to write.

With six grandchildren, Laurie finds herself concentrating her stories on the MG and YA genres. Her grandchildren like to help by offering up their imaginative ideas. Their lingo skills are often put to use. I would have never thought this about writing, but "Brah, this is so lit!"

Laurie loves to hear from readers. You can find her contact information, website details and author profile page at https://www.finch-books.com